AT THE HEARTH

STEPHANIE JEAN

At The Hearth

A Burn Me Down Collection Novella

Stephanie Jean

DEDICATION

For my former Camp Pendleton coven mates
- especially Mia and Alyssa.

Playlist

W.I.T.C.H. - Devon Cole
Season of the Witch - Lana Del Rey
Witchcraft - Frank Sinatra
Amas Veritas - Alan Silverstri
Milk & Honey - Billie Marten
To Build A Home - Rusty Clanton

Listen here:

Chapter One

There are some things that every witch worth her salt knows. One of these is the benefits of cinnamon. Prosperity, luck, abundance, you name it. There are so many ways to use cinnamon.

On this day, Selene was preparing her beginning-of-the-month rituals, most of which involved cinnamon in one form or another. She would smoke cleanse her house with a burning cinnamon stick. She would blow ground cinnamon over the threshold of her front door to welcome abundance in. She'd add a few chips to her money bowl; financial security for her family was a huge part of their general protection and safety. She would make tea that was equal parts cinnamon and lavender for creative spark and mental calm.

There were other tasks to do that did not involve cinnamon as well. Preparing her ingredients for spells throughout the month, meals throughout the week, and planning out the month ahead. Selene was the heartbeat of her house; at least that's what her husband said.

"I think we'll need to stop by the witchy supply store, Conner," she said to her little chihuahua mutt from the doorway. He looked back at her from his spot on the couch, lying flat on his side in the sun's beams. "Want to go to the store, boy?" His ears picked up, and his tail wagged a few times.

She swept the patio and left a bit of residual cinnamon powder from her hands in the little fairy garden. "Here you are, little fae," she whispered in case any sprites were listening. "You are welcome in this little garden, so enjoy it. Please stay out of my house. Thank you." She didn't have any bad fae experiences, but it was better to be safe than sorry.

Selene went back inside; Conner following her as she walked from the front door towards her altar in the back. She replaced her grimoire on the bookshelf and jotted down some notes in her book of shadows, including a shopping list, which she ripped out and folded into a square to put in her pocket.

She had on her usual mom uniform, a pair of black leggings and a crewneck. She cuffed her sleeves and pulled her hair up into a ponytail. Once bleached to be blonde, her brunette hair had grown out enough that the amber ends began at the base of her skull and cascaded down to her mid-back. She meant to touch it up, but for now, she covered her head with a baseball hat and called it good enough. "Come here, Conner!" She put his harness on him and grabbed her tote bag.

"Wallet, phone, keys, list…" she confirmed. "Poop bags, water for me, Conner's travel bowl…" She looked at her little familiar. "We could take treats with us, or we can get some while we are out." He looked back at her, panting with excitement to be in his harness for an adventure. "I'll take that as a yes."

They climbed into her car, and she made sure to tie him down appropriately to keep him safe. She held her amethyst as she turned the key, asking the powers that be to keep her safe on the roads before placing the crystal back in her center console.

"First stop, coffee. Thank the gods it's pumpkin spice season." As basic as it was, she knew that all the ingredients made for a great spell, and the warmth of the drink would keep her nervous system from getting too overwhelmed. That post-partum anxiety was still strong, even though her kids were 5 and 2. Her youngest had just started daycare, and she had recently stopped breastfeeding. She was trying her best on the daily to stay calm and not panic. "Can I also get a dog treat?" She asked. This local coffee shop also carried dog treats and cat treats for their four-legged guests.

Treats in hand, Selene drove over to the witchy supply store. It was a small house that had been half converted into a store. The front patio had fresh herb plants, suncatchers, birdbaths, and yard décor. The inside had three areas: dried herbs and candles, crystals and divination tools, and books and journals. She picked up what she needed, including some small selenite wands to put above the doors within her house. She had recently learned that it was another way to cleanse the energy from one room to the next.

She also got a few sachets to make what she called "sniff bags". Allergy season was coming, and she wanted her kiddos to be able to clear their sinuses with a small bag of herbs rather than suffering through symptoms not strong enough to warrant over-the-counter medicine. They next went to the midweek farmer's market. It was a little pop-up set up that sold seasonal fruits and veggies. She grabbed some of what she needed for the week's meals and let Conner accept loving pets from various shop owners. It was time to pick up the kids from daycare and school, so she did.

First was Juniper, at daycare. She pulled into the 15-minute parking space, cracked the windows for Conner, and went inside. The toddlers were all playing in the sandbox and with the various toys outside.

She saw her two-year-old little girl and watched her play for a moment, scooping up sand and moving it in the sandbox. Her short, strawberry blonde hair curled from sweat. When Juniper felt eyes on her, she looked up at Selene and dropped her plastic yellow shovel and ran up to her, calling out, "Mama!" Selene wrapped her up in a hug and kissed Juniper's flushed pink cheek. "Ready to go get brother?" she asked. Juniper pointed toward the gate.

Once Juniper was loaded up into her car seat with a snack cup of honey nut cereal – Selene had invoked the honey to cast a spell of sweetness – they went home. Selene moved Juniper from the car seat to a stroller and grabbed Conner's leash. They were able to walk from home to the elementary school, it was easier on her anxiety to walk with her kids than it was to deal with the car traffic in the pick-up line.

Sterling's teacher had the class lined up as he scanned the crowd for parents of his students. Since the bus kids were in front of the line, Sterling was towards the back. His dark hair was cut in a low to mid fade that Selene had learned how to do, and his blue superhero backpack was on his back. When he saw her, his smile with the missing bottom tooth widened.

Selene had learned to save the daily recap of "how was school" for dinner time. Sterling needed time to decompress and adjust from being a student to just being his five-year-old self. Their walk home was usually quiet and reflective, but sometimes, like on this day, Sterling had a lot to say.

"Mom, are we going trick or treating this year?"

"Of course we are," Selene laughed. "It's only October 1st though, baby."

He puffed out his chest. "I'm not a baby! Junie is a baby."

"No, Junie is a toddler now." Juniper was eating her cereal in her stroller and kept pushing back the shade whenever Selene tried to adjust it to cover her. "What do you want to be for Halloween this year?"

"A dragon!" Sterling continued listing different colors of dragons and what their powers were based on different variables.

When they got back home, Selene sliced up an apple and served it with peanut butter for Juniper and Sterling to share while he did homework and Juniper colored, since her homework was really just practicing motor skills.

Once Sterling's worksheets were completed, Selene got started on dinner. Every meal had the beginnings of a spell, it just needed a little intention stirred in. Tonight, they were having pesto with quick-pickled grapes, pine nuts, and chicken. She started by slicing the seedless red grapes in half and putting them in a bowl to soak in red wine vinegar. Grapes were for abundance, and the vinegar was to repel negativity. The quick pickling of the grapes while the rest of the dinner cooked made them a little sour, which was something her husband loved. She placed that bowl in the fridge and grabbed the box of chickpea pasta and her standard stainless-steel pot. "Four quarts of water to a boil," she said, measuring the water. "Add salt to taste," she dashed in some extra salt for protection as well.

As many hedge witches know, a watched pot never boils. So, she set herself to the next step, preparing the chicken. Selene had set aside some chicken breasts to thaw in the morning, and she started to cut them into cubes. She seasoned them with cumin, coriander, salt, pepper, and lemon juice, then pan-fried them on the stove with a little olive oil. By then, she was able to add the pasta to the boiling water.

"Sterling, how's the homework going, buddy?"

The kid grabbed his papers and half ran over to her with them. He was practicing writing his name. "I did all this," he said, pointing at the first four lines of his name, "I just has this left." He indicated the final line.

"You just *have* this left," his mother corrected him. "Can I watch?" He ran back over to his little table and Selene followed, sitting crisscross at his little toddler-sized table. He grabbed the pencil with his left hand, which amazed Selene as he was the only leftie in their family, excluding the potential of Juniper, who was still too small to know. Juniper was coloring on her paper. It was a page out of a coloring book. Juniper had a habit of marking once or twice on a picture and moving on. Selene was trying to get her to color in more of the page so that the coloring pages lasted longer and so Juniper would start learning how to complete tasks to the end, extending that attention span.

Not long after, Dustin came home from work. Tired and sore from a long day, he still gave his all to the kids. Selene could see the weight on his shoulders from the way he sagged in through the doorway, but he straightened up when he heard the kids. His medium-length, reddish brown beard framed his smile that reached all the way up to his maple syrup eyes.

"Daddy!" Sterling and Juniper ran to the door when they heard it open. Dustin knelt down with his lunch box, discarding it and his hat, with his arms open wide to embrace the babies. Even Conner circled around, excited that he was home.

Moments like this were Selene's bliss. Dustin's eyes met hers, and the warmth in her heart spread throughout her whole body. "Alright, kids; Mama's turn." All three of them rushed toward her. Dustin wrapped Selene in his arms and kissed her as Juniper and Sterling tried to pull them apart, each claiming, "My mommy!" and "You can't have her!".

"Okay, enough," Selene laughed, "Sterling, you and Junie should go feed Conner. He wants his dinner too." They cheered and ran out to the apartment's porch. "Welcome home," she pulled her husband back in for a hug. His deep exhale into her neck betrayed the exhaustion he was feeling. He held her tight, and she let herself feel suspended for just a moment by the love between them.

"I have some news," he said in a low voice. "We can talk about it after the kids go to sleep." Anxiety perked up in Selene's chest.

"Is everything okay?"

Dustin gave no response but a tired smile, and Selene knew, *she knew*, something was wrong. Alarm bells and sirens started going off in her head. There was a threat coming to her family, but what kind? How could she prepare against it until she knew its size, shape, and disposition?

As if he could sense her rising distress, and at this point in their marriage he usually could, Dustin interrupted her mental spiral. "We're fine. We are going to be okay." The kids clamored back in then, postponing the conversation.

Dustin and Selene had an agreement early in parenting that their rainclouds would never get their children wet. Selene had grown up too involved in all the adult stressors that her parents dealt with. She knew now that they had only wanted to prepare her for adulthood, but in reality, they had tainted too much of her childhood with it. When her grandma passed, she shouldn't have been helping budget the funeral or learning how wills work. She should have been allowed to just be sad without a lecture attached to it.

Selene announced, "Everyone wash up for dinner!" Juniper and Sterling went to their bathroom, and Dustin washed his hands in the kitchen sink. As Selene served the pasta, she noticed Dustin making himself a drink. He gave himself two shots of rum in his soda, which was only unusual because she knew, after years of marriage, that on work nights Dustin did not like to drink.

She tried not to blow it out of proportion in her mind. Some days, a hardworking man wanted a drink. There was nothing inherently *wrong* with that, and he had never given her a reason to worry about it. And yet... he had news. Mysterious and positively not joyful news. News that she was sure was going to be decidedly bad news.

As the kids climbed into their chairs, Selene drew pentagrams over their plates with her finger, blessing the food and asking the universe to shelter them from whatever storm was on the horizon.

As they ate, they each talked about their day. It was a ritual of sorts; each night at dinner, they would go around the table and share one thing you learned, one thing you were grateful for, and something you were looking forward to.

Juniper, being only two, struggled to know what to say often, and they let her answer with "I don't know" on occasion. Sterling, however, was 5. He would need to give an answer for each question. He said that he learned about the season of fall, he was grateful for his best friend Travis, and he was looking forward to Halloween so he could dress up like a dragon. Selene learned about bees at the farmers' market - and she had been wondering about having her own colony one day when they had a house - she was grateful for the witchy supply store in town, and she was looking forward to the upcoming Full Moon. Dustin said he learned about a harvest festival at a pumpkin patch, he was grateful for Selene's cooking – to which she rolled her eyes because he said this regularly – and that he was looking forward to "new opportunities". Selene tried to keep the crease from forming between her eyebrows. That response was so vague.

After dinner, they separated to their candlelit evening routines. Dustin started the dishes while Selene bathed

Juniper, and Sterling took a shower. Then the kids said good night to Dad, and Selene read them a bedtime story while Dustin showered. Tonight's story was non-fiction, picked out by Juniper, a deeply abridged biography on Ruth Bader Ginsburg. Each morning, Selene sprayed the kids' pillows with a lavender oil blend to give them peaceful rest and sweet dreams since spraying it at night was often too strong of a scent. As she bent down to tuck the kids in, she could smell the calming floral scent and asked it to keep her own anxieties calm.

Once the kids were both in bed, each given copious hugs and kisses, Selene found Dustin in their bedroom. His usually soft hair was still dark and wet from the shower, and he was in his blue plaid pajama pants and a grey T-shirt with his head in his hands. She went over and sat next to him at the foot of the bed. She put a gentle hand on his back and rubbed softly.

"Want to tell me what's going on?" she asked, even though she was scared of the answer. She braced herself for his response, whatever it could be, taking solace in the confidence that no matter what, they had each other.

Dustin's shoulders sagged as he let out a deep breath. A long, slow exhale. "I was let go at work today." There was a pause, the silence marinating in the statement. The rug had been pulled out from under them; the very bed she sat on felt like it had disappeared and she was in free fall in an abyss of uncertainty. "A bunch of us were."

Selene stood up and turned to look at him. She was trying to think. Dustin pulled out an envelope that she hadn't noticed on his other side. "They gave me two weeks severance pay and paid out all my paid time off, so our bills and everything should be covered for a little bit. And we have some money in savings, right?"

Selene's mind was starting to whirl and pick up speed as it ran rampant to find a fix, grasping at solutions only to provide one worst-case scenario after the next. "We only have enough in savings for about a month of bills and essentials since we just dipped into savings for new tires on the car, remember?"

"Well, at least we already have new tires!" He was trying to make her smile, or to offer a silver lining. When it didn't work, he stood and wrapped her in a hug. "I really believe we are going to be okay. Things are just going to be tight financially for a little bit."

"I should return the new crystals I got today," Selene said almost in a daze.

"Babe, no, it's okay. What, was it more than $50?"

"No," she replied and rested her head on his chest. Obviously it didn't make sense to return the selenite sticks and the one-dollar tumbled citrine, but she couldn't refund the coffee she had already drunk.

Dustin held her face in his hands. "I love you, Selene, but you have to believe that we are going to be fine."

"Why did they let you go? It's so out of the blue," she was getting angry at Scott Energy Solutions, Dustin's now ex-employer.

Dustin sighed heavily and sat back down on the bed. "Downsizing, and to be honest, I don't think they could afford to keep me. I'm a certified electrician, and all I really did there was make sure the A/C units and the elevator worked. They could outsource that easily for cheap. Come on, baby, let's get some rest. Tomorrow I'm going to fill out some applications, and I'll be back to work before we know it."

Selene couldn't speak, so she just nodded. They started their usual dance of getting ready for bed. Selene took a shower with her hair up because she hated going to sleep with wet hair and she was too tired to stay up drying it. She washed the day away and out of her muscles. She brushed her teeth and applied her toner and moisturizer. By the time she laid down, Dustin was already asleep.

Selene, however, had a hard time sleeping that night. She hadn't worked in six years; her full-time job had been taking care of her kids and her household. Maybe she could apply for some secretarial jobs or something. Maybe find a side hustle to help take the burden off Dustin's shoulders.

She had to admit that he was overqualified for the job he had with Scott Energy Solutions, but he had a good pay and a good schedule. It kept them in this apartment, it kept food on the table, it kept the cars maintained. And if she did start working, and he also got a job, well, what then? Sure, it was commonplace, and most Americans were two-income homes. Most had to be. Maybe if they both worked they would be able to move into a house of their own sooner, but then it was like they'd hardly ever be there. Who would drop off the kids and pick them up? Who would take them to all their doctor and dentist appointments? They'd lose their weekends together as a family, and it would turn into a two-day race of laundry and groceries and chores just to prepare for a five-day work week.

And what about her? What skills did she really have other than organizing and planning? She had no ambition to climb a corporate ladder, as if she could even get a corporate job. She had no desire to work in retail or the food industry, where the hours would be less and less likely to coincide with the kids' school schedules. What side hustle service could she even offer? Something like tarot readings online like a carnie or internet busker?

Dustin was so sure they'd be okay. She wanted to believe it too, but she also needed to be proactive. She wanted to *do* something helpful.

Chapter Two

In the morning, Selene woke up and found herself headed to the kitchen straight away. She drank a glass of water and started making breakfast for Dustin. The kids ate free breakfast at school and daycare, so she tried to take advantage of the relief those meals brought to their grocery budget. She added turmeric to the scrambled eggs – the solar properties of the turmeric should bring energy to his day, especially since he was jumping straight into job hunting. She used a cinnamon stick to stir his coffee, enchanting it to bring luck and good fortune, and deeply inhaled its earthy, sweet scent.

"I'll drive the kids this morning," Dustin offered. "You can spend your morning however you want to. Maybe take it easy, a bubble bath, and reading or painting. Whatever you want to do." He knew her so well he could see how she was already putting on her problem-solving hat. "You deserve to rest, babe. It'll be okay."

When the kids were both dressed and given a morning snack and loaded up into the car, they drove away from their two-bedroom, two-bath apartment. Selene looked around her now-quiet home. The tub in her bathroom was waiting to be filled, a bath bomb placed in it, and some calming music waiting to be played, but she had too much nervous energy. She decided that today she would take Conner for a longer walk than normal. Usually, they walked around the apartment complex before she took the kids to school, but today she would walk down to the creek. "First, we should stop by the library," she told him. His tail wagged. She gave him breakfast and went to get dressed in navy blue leggings with a matching sports bra and a zip-up pale green jacket on top. She braided her hair into two braids, put on sunscreen, and tied her shoes. "Ready, boy?" The little pup was beyond excited as she grabbed his leash and harness.

"Alright, wallet, phone, keys, water for each of us, and," she grabbed a DVD from the counter, "the library return. Let's go."

The movie had been checked out for a family movie night at home last weekend. When she returned it at the outside return window – no dogs allowed inside the library – she looked at the posting board. It was a spot for the library to post about upcoming events and local clubs and small businesses also took advantage. There was an advertisement for a lawn maintenance company, flyers for events like soap making and poetry slams, and some for sewing circles and book clubs. There was even a giant poster for the annual fall festival. Selene looked longingly at the *Witches Circle Coven* flyer.

JOIN US FOR THE FULL MOON. 21 AND OLDER TO PARTICIPATE.
TEXT JORDAN FOR INFORMATION.

Every time she came to the library, there would be one of these signs. This one looked new. She would look and want to call, want to reach out, but she never did. What if she went, but her style of mundane magic, her focus on hedge witchcraft rather than ritual magic, was somehow wrong? Or too different? She often felt inadequate as a witch when she was learning, or trying to learn, online. Social media made it seem like the Venn Diagram of the macabre and witchcraft was a singular circle. She had no delusions that she would never be gothic, collecting taxidermy, or covering her home in dark colors. It just wasn't her.

But still, she longed for community. She tried finding mom friends at the park, but the kids were never in the same age group as her kids, or they would arrive just as everyone else was leaving or vice versa.

Selene took a picture of the flyer with her phone camera, returned her DVD, and continued down to the creek. It was a mile away, then the loop she normally walked was another mile and a half, making the whole walk about 5 miles. At the halfway point, she stopped and gave herself and Conner water. She sat down in the sandy bed of the creek.

There was a gentle breeze and the long branches swayed slightly. "I don't know what we are going to do, buddy," she said, scratching Conner between the ears.

She wanted to avoid thinking about the total in the bank account, the budgeting she had planned out on repeat. There was nothing more she could do right then, and wasn't she always trying to stay present in the moment?

She remembered a simple spell to cast away worries. She picked up a smooth rock. She held it by her heart and thought about all the things she couldn't control. Employment, income, luck. She pushed each worry and fear into that little rock. Then she stood up and chucked it into the water. "May the river carry these burdens far from me."

When she got back home, she heated up some left-over pesto from the night before. Then she had what she called a "power hour" where she set a timer for 60 minutes and set her intention to tackle as much of the housework as possible. This was more than just her trying to take care of her home for herself and her family, it was an act of devotion to Hestia, the goddess of the hearth and home; it was also an offering to the spirits of her house. On the little bar of the kitchen, she lit a candle that she had anointed and dressed on the New Moon. As it burned, she unloaded the dishwasher and reloaded it with dishes from breakfast and lunch. Then she wiped down the counters and the kitchen table. She swept and moved to the laundry. She rotated the wash-er to the dryer, adding in a new load of towels from the bathrooms and kitchen. Then she started putting away the kids clothes that came out of the dryer, setting aside pajamas and clothes for the next day. Selene despised laundry, the never-ending mountain of dirty clothes that had to be washed and added to the never-ending pile of clean clothes that had to be put away. It was grueling. But, she did love the warmth of freshly dried clothes and the smell of the essential oils she had put in. This time it was a mix of clove and orange.

She realized then that she had forgotten to take something out for dinner. Selene hurriedly rushed to the freezer and grabbed some ground beef. She filled the sink with hot water to help the meat thaw in time to cook.

When the timer went off, she allowed herself to sit down and open her laptop. She stared at what she had been contemplating for a few weeks. It was an application to enter the annual autumnal art contest. Selene had wanted to enter just to put her work out there, just to take that little leap out of the fog of anonymity, not for any pressure to win. Now that they didn't have an expected income, she felt pressured to win if she entered. The cash prize of a thousand dollars would be a really big help to her family. It held more power than it did before. Was it wrong, she wondered, to want to enter just for money? Shouldn't she be creating art just for the sake of creating art?

Selene shut her laptop and pulled out her sketchbook to practice. Her preferred medium was watercolor, but she also needed to practice the principles with pencil. Her art had started as a meditative hobby. Something to do in the quiet hours when Sterling was small and

Selene had precious moments when he slept during the day. Over the years, she had grown. Dustin would complement her, calling her an artist, but she never really felt that way. "I'm just crafty," she would deflect. She used watercolor for labels on gifts, cards for anniversaries, weddings, birthdays, and décor around the house. It was something she loved to do.

Dustin came home then as she finished a sketch of Conner curled up on the couch. "Hey honey," she said, "how was the job hunt today?" It was probably too early for good news, but she was hopeful all the same.

"I went to the bank to deposit my last check, and then sat at a coffee shop researching companies and applying for a few positions," he said sitting on the couch next to her, waking Conner. "Two applications went out today. Corrections Bureau and the High School District."

"Corrections?" Selene asked, "Like, the prison?"

Dustin nodded. "There's one in the next town over, they're hiring and it's good pay but shit hours. The High School would be way better for us as far as scheduling goes, but both offer advancement and educational courses."

"Okay," she said. They were going to be okay, she had to keep reminding herself of that even when it felt like they were on the precipice of an abyss and the thought of falling in was paralyzing.

"They make applications so extensive nowadays. Not only do I have to upload a resume, but then I need to type in their questionnaire and fill out everything that's on my resume? Why do we even have to have resumes anymore? The AI that they have sort through my work experience, and no one is going to look at my uploaded document," Dustin shook his head.

"I don't know," Selene said, "but I'm proud of you for applying for jobs already."

"My brother invited me out tonight with the guys for Thursday Night Football and drinks."

"Oh, it's a school night though."

"Yeah, but it's not like I have work tomorrow," he laughed dryly, a self-depreciating laugh.

Selene bristled. "That's not funny." Dustin had the decency to look a little embarrassed. "I'm stressed about the money."

"I know, I'm sorry."

"You shouldn't joke about it."

"I shouldn't, you're right. But we're going to be fine."

She knew he was right, of course. And he should be able to go out with his brother and their friends, especially after being let go from a job. Sure she was stressed about it, but he was too, and he deserved to have some fun. She was also a little jealous. She should be able to go out with friends too. "It's just that I don't think it's fair how I never get to go out."

"I'm not stopping you, Selene. No one is." Dustin's eyes grew dark. "And you're not the one who got laid off. It was my job that was cut. It's me who has to carry that."

"We have to carry it. We're a team, Dustin."

"It's been one day."

"Yeah, I know." She was annoyed with how he kept being right. Her social circle dwindled down incrementally. First, when she got married, then when she had Sterling. Then, when she had Juniper. Each major event in her life resulted in fewer and fewer friends carrying over.

"You should go out, meet people, hang out with people," Dustin said. The image of the flyer flashed in her mind.

"There's a local coven I am thinking about joining."

"Yes! You should!" Dustin was excited for her already; she could tell. The bitter taste of the previous frustration dissipates with the change of conversation.

"I'm sorry for how I reacted to you going out," Selene apologized.

"We're good," Dustin smiled. "It's a lot of stress, and we're going to get through it. But the coven thing sounds good. Your witchcraft is important to you. You should have people to share it with."

Dustin was a very supportive husband. He had always encouraged her exploration and dedication to the craft, even if he didn't understand or partake in it.

"I'm nervous though," she whispered.

"Maybe meet up with the person in charge before meeting the whole group. Somewhere neutral like a coffee shop or something."

Selene took out her phone and drafted a message. "How's this?"

> Selene: Hey, Jordan! My name is Selene. I saw the flyer for the full moon at the library and I wanted to see if we could meet up sometime beforehand so I can introduce myself and whatnot.

"Send it," Dustin smiled. Selene hit send, locked her phone, and tucked it under her leg. "I'll pick up the kids from school so you can vibe a bit since I'll be out for the evening routine."

Ding.

Selene checked her phone; Jordan had already replied!

> Jordan: Sure, are you available Monday for a bite? Maybe lunch? My treat!

Dustin read the text too and let out a whoop. He got up and took a bite out of an apple. "I've got a good feeling about this, babe."

Selene did too. She felt a swarm of butterflies of excitement. She was reminded of the tarot card Three of Cups, a card that represented community. Maybe she was about to find hers.

Chapter Three

Jordan had wanted to meet for lunch, which was fine by Selene. They had texted back and forth and landed on meeting at a little diner in town. It had black and white checkered faux tile flooring, red vinyl booths, and an old school jukebox.

Selene: I'm here!

Selene sent the text and looked around.

Selene: I'm wearing an olive green hoodie with my hair in a ponytail.

Selene looked around and saw a woman with curly black hair and brown skin waving at her.

"Selene?" she asked. "I'm Jordan."

Jordan had one ear decorated with piercings, her acrylic nails were coffin-shaped and painted green and purple like a lavender matcha. She had a mole on her chin just left of center, and had warm eyes. She was beautiful.

"Thanks for agreeing to meet with me here. I love having an excuse to go out."

"Of course," Selene said, "thank you for the invitation."

Jordan smiled. "I'm glad you asked. And full transparency, even if you hadn't, it's customary that I meet with any potential new members before bringing them into the circle. We need to protect each other." Her eyes fluttered down at the table and she was fiddling with a ring on her pointer finger that was silver with crystals along it that Selene recognized as in alignment with the chakras. "There was a time," Jordan continued, "where we had people join who treated witchcraft like a cosplay event, who wanted to reenact their favorite movies and whatnot." Jordan let out a sigh. "And we had a few rogue fundamentalists come and try to threaten to dox our members. You get the idea." Jordan flipped over the menu. "Anyway, I started screening new members before subjecting everyone else to it."

Selene suddenly felt conflicting anxieties. First, she was nervous about being interviewed to even attend. She really didn't expect Jordan to spell out the fact that she was in the hot seat. Second, she was nervous about being in danger from being in a coven by those outside. But at the same time, she was relieved that there were safety precautions in place.

They looked over the menus until a waiter came by for their order.

"I'll have a cheesesteak sandwich and a lemonade. Can you swap the fries for potato wedges? Thanks."

Selene glanced quickly at the prices and made sure her order wouldn't be more than Jordan's. Sure, Jordan offered to pay, but Selene wasn't going to take advantage of that. "I'll have the classic cheeseburger. Cheddar cheese."

"How do you want that cooked?" The waiter asked.

"Medium, please."

"And for your drink?"

"I'll stick with just water, thanks." Selene gestured to the two waters on the table.

"And fries are okay?"

"Yeah, thanks."

"Alright, ladies. I'll be right back with those." The waiter scribbled notes on the notepad and walked away.

Jordan leaned back in her booth. "So, tell me about yourself."

Oh no. Selene held back a groan at the broadness of the question. Her entire sense of self felt like a blank canvas. "Ah," she started, having no idea where to go with the sentence. What to say? Where to start? "I'm a wife and mother to two kids, and... uh," she cringed a little at how bland she felt. "I have a dog named Conner."

"And what can you tell me about your journey with the craft?"

Thank the gods, she thought, *a direct question.*

"Well, I started a few years ago." She paused, calculating. "Ten years ago, actually. So yeah, a decade. I had found a website about Wicca and read the Rede and it resonated, which led to me feeling drawn to learn more about magic. I've just kind of looked things up and tried things out. Mostly hedge witchcraft. Mostly by myself." Selene ran her clammy palms along the top of her thighs under the table. "I don't really do rituals in like, a formal sense. It feels a little unnatural to me when I'm just by myself in my apartment. But I have small rituals and routines that I do." Selene sipped her water.

"So, do you consider yourself a Wiccan, a pagan, a witch? There are a lot of labels, and they don't matter to everyone, but some people are more… particular."

Selene wasn't sure if this was a make-or-break question in the interview. Was Jordan trying to hint to Selene that these labels were superfluous, or was she the kind to hold a lot of weight with them? "Um, just a witch. Wicca wasn't really a fit for me, and there are so many gods out there that to narrow it down to who to follow in which pantheon is…" Selene let out a whistle. "It's intimidating. I don't know. I never really looked that far into it. I just do little things like cooking spells and bath rituals, blessings and protections for my kids. Casual everyday things. I like Hestia a lot, though."

Jordan smiled wide. "That's awesome." Selene's shoulders relaxed a little from the acceptance. "Our coven is eclectic. Some pagans, some not, a couple of wiccans, and one devotee of Lilith. Everyone has different levels of experience. We usually follow the Wiccan format of rituals, but everyone invokes their own gods, goddesses, ancestors, or spirits. We'll do some energy work as a group and then our own variations of the same spells, and then eat." Jordan laughed. "We might drink or smoke after, but only once the circle is opened at the end. You shouldn't cast under the influence, especially in a group."

"Oh?" Selene asked. "Sounds like there's a story there."

Jordan chuckled. "Let's just say some girls came up once and they were trying to summon something to possess one of their ex-boyfriends and ruin his life. Another member thought it would be funny to do, and the girls had been, shall we say, *supplementing* her courage. They tried astral projection and one of them started hallucinating that a devil was crawling out of the floor, and the other thought the first girl was having a seizure." At Selene's horrified expression, Jordan quickly clarified. "No, no. She was fine, they all were. They just got scared, and the one girl peed her pants. Literally. I had to wash the carpet there fifty times before I felt confident it was clean enough."

Just then, their food arrived. The waiter placed the meals in front of them, and Selene admired the little flag on a toothpick that had a cartoon chef giving a thumbs up. "Wow, this looks great, thanks!" Jordan beamed at the waiter and then returned to talking to Selene. "I'll tell you a little about myself. I'm 34 years old, and I've been the coven leader here for the last three years, since my little boy was six months old. My husband is a truck driver for SupplyCorp and he's gone a lot of the time. I started my practice as a kid because I was raised by a hedge witch." Her eye had a glimmer in it and Selene felt a flutter of connection. "She was a pagan who honored the home, much like you." Jordan smiled, and Selene didn't know what to say. "She would always make sure we had fresh flowers on the table when she bought groceries. She would say, 'When the flowers wilt, I know it's time to buy more groceries.'" Jordan chuckled. "I know now that it was more of an ADHD brain hack than anything magical; that groceries put away were out of sight and out of mind."

"That's a great hack, though," Selene said. "I think those neurodivergent tips are great."

"Are you neurodivergent?"

"Not on paper," Selene said, "and I'm not trying to self-diagnose or anything. I don't think I am, but a lot of people have told me that I probably fit the ticket." Her husband used to joke about it. Her parents were of the belief that she was fine, but in her early adulthood, she had many neurodivergent friends who would tell her that she was the same flavor of spicy as they were. "I don't know, and to be honest, I'm not really worried about it."

Jordan nodded as she ate a potato wedge.

"But in any case, I think I might start bringing in flowers more. If nothing else, it would be a nice passive enchantment depending on the flowers."

As they ate, the conversation turned to their spouses and kids. Selene found that she had relaxed to a point of familiarity and comfort. It was as if she and Jordan had been friends for a few years, not an hour or so.

After paying for the check, the pair stood in the parking lot. Jordan clapped her hands together with finality. "Well, I would love it if you joined us for the Full Moon. You can decide after if you want to fully join the coven as a member. If you decide it's not for you, that's totally okay, but I hope you like it because I like you."

Selene was giddy. "Thank you! I'm really excited, and I like you too!"

"I feel like this is the start of a great friendship, Selene. Is there anything I can do for you before the ritual?"

She hesitated. In their conversation about their families, Selene had mentioned that Dustin was between jobs. Should she ask for help manifesting a new job for him? Was that tacky at the first meeting? Jordan was a coven leader, and she was probably asked to expend her energy on behalf of others. Did she really want to add herself to that list already?

"I'm not sure," was all she could think to say. "If I think of something, I'll let you know."

"Well, don't hesitate to reach out. You have my number. If you want to hang out again, just let me know when! I need to go pick up my son from my sister-in-law." Jordan gave Selene a hug and walked toward her car.

Chapter Four

W hen she got back home, Selene decided to give herself a reading with an oracle deck. She drew a card that represented "Attunement". She annotated it in her book of shadows, journaling:

I met with a coven leader today. Her name is Jordan. She invited me to the Full Moon circle. I'm excited and nervous – then I came home and pulled the "Attunement" card from my oracle deck. Attune to what? The group? Myself? The guidebook that came with the deck says that this card suggests attuning to a tool or skill. Maybe it's about the contest? About painting? What should I even paint for the contest?

Then, it was time to go get the kids. Juniper had an accident at school during naptime, so Selene needed to take the bedding home and wash it before the next day. Sterling had a good day, but fell at recess and scraped his elbow. "Mom," he said on their walk home, "I need a new Band-Aid. This one is dirty." Selene looked at it and saw what looked like pencil marks on the woven tan bandage.

"What happened to it?" she asked.

"Travis tried to sign it like a cast, but it didn't work, so now it's dirty and Finley said it was gross because a dirty bandage means you don't take baths."

Selene exhaled with a smile. "It's fine, kiddo. Just leave it alone and we'll put another one on tonight after your shower." He did not take that well. Sterling kicked a rock on the sidewalk and pouted, "You're mean, Mom."

"Woah, okay." That stung, but Selene tried to take a deep breath before reacting. How could she expect her five-year-old to regulate his emotions unless she showed him? "Come here," she said. "Juniper, wait one minute." Juniper stood and watched as Selene squatted down to their level. Sterling was still pouting. "I am not being mean, the bandage is fine. I already told you, you'll get a new one tonight. You'll just have to wait until then."

"But I don't want to wait, I just want a new one."

"Take a deep breath with me," Selene said. "Mommy has some big feelings right now, so I'm going to breathe. Are you having some big feelings, too? Junie, want to breathe with us?" Juniper nodded and held Sterling's hand. They took three deep breaths together. "Okay," Selene continued, "so we will wait until tonight so we can get a new bandage, okay? Getting one between now and your shower is wasteful."

Sterling nodded but said, "It's not fair."

Selene sighed, "Yeah, I get that."

They made it home as usual, and Selene started preparing the house for dinner. She went through her mental checklist of her afternoon chores. *Empty the trash, take out all the ingredients for dinner, water the plants, check the mail, send the kids to feed the dog.*

When Dustin came home, he handed her a bouquet of orange and yellow carnations. "You are my lucky charm," he said, giving her a hug. "You gave me that talisman and baby, today it worked."

"Shut up, did you get a job?"

He laughed, "Okay, let's not get out crazy. I got an interview!"

Selene squealed and gave him another hug. "That's amazing! Where? When?" She turned to stir the chicken with the honey orange sauce she was preparing for dinner.

"It's on Friday with the Corrections Department." He leaned against the counter next to the stovetop. "It's a preliminary interview, and I have to take a skills test and pass a drug test. And get this, it's a group interview."

"A group interview? Like, all of you in the same room?" Dustin nodded and Selene was amazed in an intimidated way. "That's... intense."

"Yeah. I think he said it would be eight of us in there."

Selene checked on the rice she had begun cooking earlier and started the frozen vegetables in the microwave. "So, what can I do to help? Do you need to prepare? Should I look up interview questions?"

Dustin ran his hand up and down her arm. "No, I'll be okay." He then picked up the bouquet and grabbed some scissors to cut the stems and place them in a vase. "Tell me about your meeting today!"

So, she did. "Jordan is really nice, and I'm looking forward to the Full Moon. It's going to be cool to see how a coven works."

"That's good that you're excited, I think it's important that you have something like this." He placed the carnations in the vase with some water and then placed it on the center of the table as he announced to the kids that it was almost time for dinner.

Selene hoped Dustin would get the job, but she recognized what he had said. This was a preliminary interview, which meant this would be a multiple step process. If he did make it past this interview, how many more steps were there until the job was secured? How long would it take? And could they survive that long on what they had in savings?

After Juniper and Sterling were in bed, Selene went to pull out her sketchpad to make a list of potential paintings for the Art Contest.

1. *Conner at the creek*

2. *Kitchen mid-meal prep*

3. *Something with the moon?*

She couldn't think. There were too many ideas and not enough time to do all of them before the contest. She needed whatever she picked for her watercolor rendering to be good enough to win and her ideas felt too small. Too quaint. They were intimate things to her, but who else would care about the subject? There had to be something universally meaningful. And at the same time, these were huge ideas. These watercolors would be large scenes of still life moments, rather than something small and simple. Huge undertakings that would require quite a bit of time to get the details right, and if she made a mistake and needed to restart... Well, then what? There definitely wasn't enough time to get all of them done and pick the best one. Selene chastised herself for not starting sooner.

With her phone, she snapped a photo of her tarot cards next to the carnations so she could reference the shadows and relation of each item to one another if she didn't finish the drawing tonight. She started sketching the image while she let her mind wander. Was Dustin ready for the interview? She should iron his outfit for him. The interview, more specifically the job search in general, was something, again, that was out of her control. She wanted to help, somehow. Something more tangible and impactful than a lucky charm talisman.

"What are you doing out here?" Dustin asked.

"Sketching." She had been curled up on a chair at the table. She stretched her legs under the table and rolled her neck. "And thinking."

Dustin sat next to her on another chair, and Selene closed her sketchbook and held his hand. "What are you thinking about?"

"I don't feel like I'm doing enough to help you."

"What?"

Selene shrugged. "I don't make any money. We are a single-income family in a dual-income world. And we don't even have an income right now."

"But what you do is so important for the family. You are the heart of this home, Selene."

Selene gave him a look. "I appreciate that, but I still feel this inadequacy. Shouldn't I be making some financially positive impact? I see all these other stay-at-home moms online with their side hustles and their content creation, and all I can think is 'why can't I seem to manage to do that too?' They take that income and put it toward their families and themselves and I just feel like I'm not measuring up."

"Sweetheart." Dustin's thumb swiped along the top of her knuckles. "You can't believe someone's internet feed to be indicative of real life."

Selene chewed on her inner cheek. "I love being a stay-at-home mom. I love that my primary focus is our family, and I love that you provide for us so I can explore personal passions like cooking and art. But I also feel like maybe I should be, I don't know, aspiring for more? Striving to be a corporate baddie or small business owner." Selene groaned. "But I don't want to. I don't want to strain and strive. I just want to live gently, raise good people, and make art."

"So don't change, honey. We are going to be just fine."

"There is one thing," Selene started, but Dustin leaned in and kissed her, interrupting what he thought was her spiraling. She decided to wait to tell him about the contest. She wasn't even convinced she would apply for it yet.

Chapter Five

S elene went through the next few days the same as always. She made the meals, cleaned the apartment, and rotated and put away laundry. She took Conner out for a walk, twice, and started painting. She was working on a piece that could be a background for Sterling's puppet shows. It was more for practice than anything, not quite right for the contest, she thought. Her watercolor supplies were, from the outside, a mix of quality. She had cheap paints, cheap watercolor paper, which was more expensive than regular paper but inexpensive as far as watercolor papers went, and a few nice brushes. When Selene had first looked into watercolor, she learned that one thing to splurge on was the brushes. You could make any shade, tone, or tint of color you wanted using a basic kindergarten set and color theory. But bad brushes made bad strokes.

She dragged the green pigment along the inside of what would be the leaves of trees, pulling the water and pigment down the curve and in toward the center of the shape. What was she going to paint for the contest? These cartoonish backdrops were great for her five-year-old, but up against who knows how many talented people... Selene shook her head and tried to fight off the anxieties. When she was done with the green leaves, she walked away to let the layer dry.

In the living room, she saw the flowers that Dustin had brought home. They had bloomed fully and looked amazing. Selene snapped a picture on her phone and sent it to Jordan.

Selene: Kitchen table flowers. My husband brought these home after our meeting. It's like he knew we had been talking about it.

Jordan replied with a laughing emoji and a "That's so perfect" text.

On the morning of Dustin's interview, Selene made his breakfast of scrambled eggs with cheese and sausage with a side of buttered toast with raspberry jam.

Over the week, Selene had pre-made pancakes and frozen them to reheat as a little snack for the kids on their way to school. She warmed one up for each of them and placed them by the backpacks.

"Sterling!" Selene called through the apartment, "Are you getting dressed?"

"Yes!" He called back.

Selene had gotten Juniper dressed before making breakfast, and now she took her into the bathroom. "Alright, let's do your hair, pretty girl." She brushed Juniper's hair into two pigtails that barely reached the toddler's shoulders. "Are you excited to go to school today?" she asked.

"Yeah, I like school," Juniper said. "I want to play sandbox."

"Oo, sandbox is fun."

Then Sterling came into the bathroom, too. "I don't play sandbox at my school. We play *The Floor is Lava*."

Selene transitioned to combing Sterling's hair. "That game is really fun, too." Selene encouraged. "Okay, let's go put on our shoes and jackets."

"I don't want to wear my jacket," Sterling started to whine.

"Me either," Juniper followed her big brother's lead.

"Well, that's too bad. Jackets, or no pancake on the way to school."

"No!" the kids yelled in unison, and they scampered to their room to get their shoes on.

"Hey, babe!" Dustin called, "I can't find my black socks. Do you think it'd be okay if I just wore white ones?"

Selene took a deep breath and went into their room. "The socks are right here, I laid them out for you." She pointed at the space on top of his dresser, but it was empty. "Crap."

"I thought I saw them earlier too," Dustin said. "But when I came out of the bathroom after shaving, I couldn't find it."

Selene looked around. Had some kind of fae creature or sprite gotten into her house? They were known tricksters. "Hold on," she went outside to their little patio. Conner jumped around, thinking she was going to take him for a walk. "Not yet, buddy." She had a small fairy garden on the patio as a space for the fae to rest without needing to come inside and mess with her family. It was a little dirty, and the water cup was empty. She wiped off the tiny chairs, filled the small water bowl, and added a little plastic gem that had come off one of Juniper's art projects. "Here you go, fae. Please stay out of my house."

Then she went back inside toward the bedroom. "I found them!" Dustin announced as she crossed the doorway.

"Great. Your breakfast is ready. I'm going to take the kids to school." She gave him a kiss and held his face in her hands. "Good luck today, I love you and I am so proud to be your wife."

"Thanks, babe. I love you too."

"Oh, take this." She handed him a green aventurine tumbled crystal. "Keep it in your pocket."

Dustin smiled and slid the stone into his front pants pocket. "I'll see you tonight. Pumpkin patch tomorrow?"

Selene smiled. "Yes."

They had decided earlier in the week to have something to look forward to after the interview. Something fun for the family that would be a light at the end of the tunnel of the day. As Sterling buckled himself in and Selene buckled Juniper's car seat, she handed them each their pancakes.

"Pumpkin Spice Pancakes!" They cheered.

"Mama, that's a star," Juniper said, indicating the Pentagram Selene had branded into each pancake.

"Yes, baby," she said. "It's a star of all the elements. Fire, Water, Earth, and Air. The top one is Spirit. All the elements make up everything around us. They make up each part of us."

Juniper just stared at the star for a moment and took a bite out of the pancake. Selene wasn't sure how to share her beliefs with her kids. She wanted them to be curious, explore different beliefs, and find what resonated with them the best. But she also wanted to share her practices with them. Maybe they would grow up and not practice witchcraft, that was fine, but at least she didn't hide it from them.

Selene tried to keep everything as natural as possible. She honored the sabbats because nature was changing, which was something they could see was happening. She didn't want to force her kids into worshipping any deities.

Amethyst in the console and sunglasses on, they listened to the radio on the way to school. She dropped off Sterling first, then took Juniper to daycare, which was a 20-minute drive away. On the way back, she stopped at a small grocery market to pick up a few things for dinner that night. It was going to be a casserole kind of night, and she needed cream of mushroom soup and mixed vegetables.

Then, she needed to pick up prescriptions from the pharmacy, drop off a package at the post office, and swing by the dollar store for a new box of crayons for the kids.

When Selene took Conner on a walk, she had a sudden spark of inspiration. A concept for a watercolor that she really wanted to make, and maybe enter it in the contest.

She started sketching back in her apartment and lost track of time. She worked on the piece well past lunchtime and only realized because her alarm went off that she needed to leave soon to pick up the kids. She sat up from where she had been working at the kitchen table, took a picture of the still life she had set up for later reference, and packed up her things.

That night at dinner, they went around the table. Dustin hadn't told her an update about the interview because he said he wanted to save it for the table. Juniper learned *Twinkle Twinkle* and attempted to sing it to them, she was grateful for "Mommy, Daddy, and Sterling, and Conner," which was pronounced with a P so it sounded like Ponner, and when asked what she was looking forward to, she shrugged and said, "I eat my food!"

Sterling had learned about scarecrows, was grateful for Josiah's birthday at school because he got a cupcake, and he was looking forward to carving a pumpkin. Selene had learned that the Full Moon coming up was called a Hunter's Moon, she was grateful for her watercolor painting, and she was looking forward to finishing the piece she had started. Dustin's turn was next, and Selene felt her core tighten with anticipation. "I learned that there are a lot of steps in this application process for the Corrections Department," he started.

"What does that mean?" Sterling asked.

"It's a new job I'm trying to get. They want to make sure they hire the right person."

"Are you the right person?" Sterling asked again.

"I want to be, but…" Dustin trailed off. "I know I am a hard worker. I don't know if that means I'm the right person for them, but I know I can do hard things."

"And you're big and strong," Sterling continued, reciting some affirmations that they said throughout the day.

Dustin smiled. "Yeah, thanks, kid."

Selene wanted him to continue and typically tried to model not interrupting to her kids, but she had to know. "So, how was it?"

"I got moved on to the next phase. Which is one thing I'm grateful for. It was a tough room; there were a lot of people in there who had more experience or more applicable experience than I do." Dustin shrugged and took a sip of his drink. "But the thing I'm looking forward to is that I have another interview with the school district on Thursday."

"Oh yay!" Selene said, and the kids cheered as well. "That's good, that's really good." Selene had no doubt that her husband would be great if he were to be hired by the Corrections Department, but she felt better knowing there were options. "That's good. It's good not to put all your eggs in one basket."

"Because eggs only go in baskets at Easter," Sterling said, misunderstanding the phrase.

"No," Selene laughed, "it's an expression. It means it's better to try for a few things than only one."

"And the school pays less, but the hours would be better," Dustin said. Then shook his head, money things were not something they needed to burden their kids with when they were this little. "Wouldn't you rather have Daddy home at dinner time?" he asked the kids.

Sterling nodded, and Juniper wasn't paying attention. Selene took Dustin's hand in hers, "No matter what happens, we'll be okay. We'll make time."

CHAPTER SIX

S aturday morning, Selene woke up early to start outlining her sketch on the watercolor paper. She did so very faintly with a pencil. She started with the foreground while sketching. The tarot cards, the crystals, the candle, and the bouquet of flowers in the middle space. Then the background, the end of the table, and the chairs at the other end. She had sketched the entire still-life scene. The primary card was the Ten of Pentacles. She hadn't drawn the details of the card yet because she wanted to design one herself.

Next, she started testing colors on a scrap piece of watercolor paper, trying to mix the right amount of red, yellow, and orange to get the carnations' colors just right. She kept trying to get pink from using less and less red pigment since her watercolor set did not have white.

The only colors at her disposal were the ones you'd find in an elementary school. Red, Orange, Yellow, Green, Blue, Purple, Brown, and Black. When she first started learning about watercolor, one of the rules she abided by was to never use black pigment; shadows were made of contrasting colors with a lower chroma, and it would look more realistic than using black for shading. The only exception to this was when she was painting a black item, but she hadn't run into that yet. She would still use a combination of blue, orange, and brown to get a dark enough color.

Sterling came out of the kids' room, rubbing his eyes. "Are we going to the pumpkin patch today?" he asked.

"Yes, we are, good morning."

"Good morning." Sterling stood there, still half asleep.

Selene looked at the clock and saw it was seven in the morning. "Are you ready to wake up?" Sterling shook his head. "Go back to bed; I'll come get you in a little bit." When his door closed, she packed up her things and got the table cleared for breakfast. She put all her watercolor things in a basket and stored them on the top shelf of a cabinet in the hallway, including her board with the stretched paper that had been stapled down.

Then she went into her room to get dressed. Dustin was still in bed, so she opened the blinds to let the natural light into the room. "Good morning, honey," she said. "It's time to get up."

She leaned down to kiss him, and he wrapped his arms around her and twisted like a crocodile, pulling her onto the bed and cuddling her. "Hey!" she protested playfully.

"I just want to be close to you, is that a crime?" Dustin's voice was deep and rough still from sleep. He nuzzled into her neck. "You're warm," he said.

"And I need to make breakfast. Sterling was already up."

Dustin let out a half-hearted groan. "Fine," he said in a dramatically defeated way. "Leave me, abandon your husband who only wants to be near you."

Selene laughed. "Get off me."

Dustin made no attempt to do so; in fact, his strong arms held her tighter to him. "Go ahead, go," he teased.

Selene went to tickle his underarms. A low blow, to be sure, but effective. He recoiled, letting out an "Ah!" but she couldn't get off the bed fast enough. He repositioned and pinned her again. "So that's the way you treat your poor, defenseless husband? You cruel witch." Then he started tickling her neck, her thighs. To Selene's misfortune, she was incredibly ticklish. "You did this," he teased her, and she laughed.

"Ah, no! Stop, please," she tried to keep from squealing with laughter. "You're going to wake up the kids," she tried to argue.

"You're the one being loud," he taunted, but his tickling ceased.

"Get up," she repeated. "We are going to have a good day."

She rolled out of bed and walked to the bathroom. Undoing the braid she slept in, she combed her fingers through her hair, the waves shades of grown-out dye. She grabbed the clear glass spray bottle filled with rose quartz-infused moon water from the last full moon and sprayed her hair, then shook it to release any stagnant energy. She washed her face and used a toner that contained rose water before applying moisturizer. As she let the moisturizer absorb and dry, she moved back out toward her closet. Her pajamas were a set of black shorts and a soft heather grey top that read "Good Mood" in thin white letters. She put on a pair of skinny jeans – she knew they were terminally millennial at this point, but who cared? As far as she and Taylor Swift were concerned, "Old habits die screaming." She put on socks and black running shoes, then a medium, mossy green colored cropped sweatshirt. Back in the bathroom, she reached past Dustin, who was now combing out his short beard, and grabbed her facial sunscreen. "You and your lotions and potions." He smiled. She rolled her eyes playfully.

Their bathrooms were small, and each one was connected directly to one of the two bedrooms. There was one sink, a medicine cabinet, a large mirror, next to no counter space, a toilet, and a combination shower and bath. Selene had opted for a transparent but frosted shower curtain so the room felt brighter and light would come into the shower since there were no windows. Thankfully, she only used a handful of makeup products. She used to have a lot more; she would experiment with eyeshadows and different lip colors, but after Sterling was born, she didn't find joy in makeup in the same way. It was one of the easier things to simplify in her transition into motherhood.

Her daily makeup look started with brow gel, followed by eyeshadow. She only had one small eyeshadow palette of three shades of pink: one dark, one light, and one shimmer. Then she applied mascara, the bottle had sigils all over it from an old glamour spell where she wanted to see things that were pretty and be seen as alert. Then she brushed on some blush, followed by a crème-based highlight on her cheekbones. She added a tinted lip balm and called it a day.

Her hair she decided to put up with a claw clip. Even though her waves were cooperating now, she anticipated running around after Sterling and Juniper all day would eventually require her to tie down her locks. Might as well get ahead of it.

Last to do were accessories: her pentagram necklace, a pair of amethyst stud earrings, and her watch. She grabbed her crossbody bag, inside containing the minimum: phone, wallet, lip balm, hand sanitizer, gum, a nail file, a piece of black tourmaline, and her sunglasses.

Everything else her kids could possibly need was in the diaper bag. Sterling had long since stopped needing the diaper bag, and Juniper was close to being fully potty trained, but there were still accidents that happened. Two changes of clothes, a lot of wipes, and spare dog poop bags in case she needed to bag up dirty/wet clothes.

After the kids were up and dressed, fed, and loaded into the car, Selene gave Conner a treat from his container before locking up the apartment. The drive to the pumpkin patch was about thirty minutes. Most of the drive, they listened to the radio. Selene had decided around the time Sterling was three that she didn't want to play DJ to the whims of a toddler. He would complain, "I don't like this song" to anything she would play. Eventually, enough was enough. "It's the radio," she told him, "I can't control what song they play."

Dustin had mentioned that they could say it was the radio even if it was one of their playlists, but she had grown to enjoy releasing that executive function over to the radio dial. She didn't need to think about which playlist to listen to or what vibe she wanted. She didn't need to worry about any of it. She just kept it on the local country music station.

When they pulled up to the pumpkin patch, it was already packed with people. "It's busier than I thought it would be," she said as Dustin put the car in park. "I wonder if we should just leave the wagon so it's not in the way."

"I'll deal with the wagon," he said. "We are about to get a bunch of pumpkins, and I'm not carrying them all back to the car. And this way the kids can sit if they want to."

The pumpkin patch was just one part of the farm. This was where the Autumnal Festival was held, where the presentation and awards for the Art Contest would take place. They paid the entry fee, and each ticket came with a pumpkin of your choosing. There were the pumpkins, yes, but also food stands, farmers market type booths, a tractor ride that gave the history of

the farm, a smaller tractor ride for kids, bounce houses, sunflower fields to take pictures in, a corn maze,
a petting zoo, and turf slides. Sterling wanted to try
everything and run everywhere at once.

"Hold on, kiddo," Dustin said. "Mama, what would you
like to do first?" He directed the question at Selene.

"I think I want to look at the petting zoo, then the
games and rides, then we can grab some lunch, corn
maze, pick up pumpkins, and head home?"

Dustin nodded, then looked at Sterling and Juniper.
"You guys understand the game plan?" Sterling nodded.
Juniper was only 2 and wasn't really paying attention,
more fascinated with the entry stamp on her hand of a
purple bat.

They walked through the petting zoo. Sterling's favorite was the goats. "I want a goat!" he declared. "Can
we take one home?"

"Where would he sleep?" Selene asked.

"He could sleep on the couch!"

Dustin and Selene laughed as they pushed along, Juniper in the wagon, Sterling dashing from one pen to
another down the dirt path that swooped around in a
large U shape.

The path widened to the play area. There was so
much to do, carnival-style games like ring toss and mini
basketball were lined up in a row, but Sterling wanted
to do the turf sledding first. It was a large mound of dirt
with synthetic grass on top, about 20 to 30 feet tall, and
it came down in a nice semi-steep slope. The farm pro-

vided large pieces of cardboard. "Come on, kids!" Dustin grabbed Juniper and held Sterling's hand over to the cardboard. They selected two large boards and climbed the hill. At the top, Dustin showed Sterling how to lay the board down and sit on it. Sterling sat on one, and Dustin was on the other, with Juniper on his lap. Then, Dustin put a hand on the back of Sterling's board and gave it a good shove. Sterling started sliding down the slope, an elated shriek coming from his open-mouthed grin. Dustin pushed off behind, and Juniper looked just as excited, giggling all the way.

"Again, again!" Sterling jumped up immediately, not even fully coming to a stop. "Mom, did you see me do that?"

"I did," Selene smiled. "You're so fast!"

"Okay, let's go again," Dustin said. "You okay, mama?"

Selene nodded. "I'm good. I'm going to go look at these signs over here." She pointed to some bulletin boards posted behind the cardboard stacks. There were the rules for the turf sledding, the hours of the pumpkin patch, and announcements for Spooky Court, a sort of "homecoming queen" style pageant. And there it was. The Art Contest. She had been looking at the same flyer on her laptop, but on the bottom of this flyer, it said **Register by October 20th**. Selene looked at her phone. It was already the 12th! She only had eight days to register, and she hadn't even talked to Dustin about it yet. The registration fee was only five dollars, but if he didn't get a job soon, she shouldn't gamble any money on a potential loss. This day was already going to be a burden on their finances just because of the park entry and the food.

She tried to calm herself down; they had talked about this. It was going to be okay. This was an expense they had agreed to. Something good for the family. Selene decided to talk to Dustin about it later.

The kids went on the little tractor ride, and Dustin and Selene took pictures. For lunch, they each got a corndog and shared two fries. They ate as they wandered the corn maze, both kids in the wagon. Juniper was peeling the breading off her corndog and only ate the meat inside once all the batter and the fries had been eaten.

"Imagine being here, just us," Dustin said. "No one else around. Might get a little... carried away, if you know what I mean." He waggled his eyebrows at her. She laughed and rolled her eyes.

"Oh, whatever. You love the comfort of our bed."

He sighed wistfully. "I do, but a guy can dream."

"About a corn maze?"

He lowered his voice and leaned in to say, "About you in a little sundress with nothing underneath in a corn maze."

"We made it!" Sterling cheered, interrupting the grown-ups as the exit appeared.

The exit of the corn maze dumped them right at the pumpkin area. There were countless pumpkins scattered around a huge area. They were in rows, in wheelbarrows, on top of hay bales, and in piles. Some were as small as a square tissue box, some were as large as a tote bag.

"Alright, kids, go pick one each!" Dustin helped Juniper out of the wagon. "Sterling, stay with Junie." They watched the kids run into the sea of pumpkins.

"You stay with the wagon, I'll go help," Selene said.

Sterling was trying to pick out Juniper's first. She would grab one, and then see another and immediately grab that one. Sterling's eyes were big.

"We need to find the biggest pumpkins we ever saw!" he exclaimed.

"Just get some smaller ones, remember we are getting four of them and they need to fit by our front door."

Sterling didn't like that idea, but he obeyed. He had to make sure his was at least bigger than Juniper's, though. Then, Selene picked one out for herself. It was decently sized, about the size of a basketball. When they returned to Dustin, he had picked one out too, and it was already in the wagon.

"Four pumpkins," Sterling said, instructing Juniper. "One, two, three, four." Juniper watched him and repeated, "Four!"

That night, when they got home, Dustin set up the table to carve the pumpkins. Selene had a frozen pizza, so she put it in the oven for an easy dinner tonight.

"First, we have to design the faces."

On scraps of old paper, Selene gave them each a crayon, and they started designing. She helped Juniper by making her a menu of shapes. "What kind of eyes should your pumpkin have?" Juniper pointed at a circle and a triangle. Selene drew the shapes as eyes lower on the paper. "And should your pumpkin smile or frown or neither?"

Juniper pointed at the one with a rectangle for a mouth, "That one, mommy!"

"Mine is going to have a big mouth," Sterling said, drawing on his paper. "With lots of teeth, like Dad's!"

Selene glanced over at Dustin's design. It was like a lightning scar more than a mouth. "I was thinking of flames," Dustin said.

"How many teeth should your pumpkin have?" Selene asked Juniper. "Um, one."

Selene showed Juniper the picture, and once she gave the nod of approval, Selene copied it onto the smallest pumpkin.

Dustin carved the tops of the pumpkins, removing the stems. "Yay, guts!" Dustin cheered. Sterling cheered too, but Juniper recoiled.

"Eww daddy, those boogies," she said.

"You need to help clean them out," Dustin told her. Sterling was already elbow deep into a pumpkin, pulling out the seeds and guts. "Then we can finish his face and put him outside."

Juniper grabbed a handful and then turned to Selene. "My hands is sticky."

"I know, baby, let's get the gunk out."

It went on like that for a while. Juniper wanted to wash her hands after each small handful of seeds was removed.

Selene drew her pumpkin's face and started cutting it out, then Juniper's. Dustin did his own and Sterling's. When they finished, the oven timer was beeping.

"Time to eat, go wash up." Dustin went to help the kids while Selene quickly cleared the pumpkin guts filled newspaper covering from the table. She placed the four Jack o' lanterns on the bar facing them, set the table for dinner, and started thinking about how her art project was ready for her to start painting.

Chapter Seven

Selene stared at her canvas. It needed paint. She needed to start, but she was nervous. She kept sampling color combinations on scrap paper. Dustin was playing a video game when he noticed her stillness.

"You okay over there?" he asked from the couch. She was sitting at the dining table just in his line of sight.

She got up and went into the kitchen to grab some drinking water. "Yeah, I just... I'm stuck."

"Why?"

Selene sighed. "There's a lot of pressure. It has to be perfect."

Dustin paused his game and came over to her, grabbing a chocolate chip cookie from the jar and splitting it, offering her half. She took it. He waited, knowing there was more she wanted to say.

Selene took a small bite of the cookie. She had made them as a small love spell to remind her family that they were loved and to welcome love in.

"I want to enter the art contest," she confessed in the silence.

"Alright," he said as if she had mentioned something inconsequential. As if she had said, "I think I want to wear my hair down tomorrow instead of up." To add to the vibe of nonchalance, he continued. "You should. Is that what's making you freak out?"

Selene groaned weakly. "Yes. It's a contest. There's an entry fee…"

"How much is it?" he interrupted.

"Five dollars."

"Pfft," he waved his hand dismissively. "Easy. Do it."

"But our budget is so tight and-"

"Do it," he interrupted her again. "We can pay five dollars for you to share something you're passionate about; to do something you enjoy. You don't do enough for yourself, babe."

She wanted to argue, but couldn't think of something to say. "There's a cash prize," she said instead, "and if I win it, I will be helping the family."

Dustin put his hands on her shoulders and looked directly into her eyes. "You do so much for the family, Selene. I don't know how many times I need to remind you that, but I will continue to do so. You keep everything running, and you are a great mom to our kids. They adore you and learn a lot from you every day. You are the best wife in the world. I wouldn't want anyone else by my side in these highs and lows. I'm proud of you for everything you do. I'm grateful. If my wife wants to enter an art contest, then by all means, you *deserve* to." He wrapped her in a hug when her eyes started to water. "And would it be cool to win a cash prize? Sure. Of course. But who cares? Just make something you're proud of and let us be proud of you."

Selene took a deep breath in, then sat back down at her project. Maybe she should pull an oracle card. From her deck, she shuffled and drew the card representing "Community". The image was of some hippos lying in the mud together. Selene thought of Jordan and the upcoming Full Moon circle in two days.

"The Full Moon is on Monday," she said aloud. Dustin was back to playing his game.

"That's right. Are you excited?"

Selene dipped her brush into the water and started adding pigment to the background of the rendering. "I am. I think maybe I need to get out of my own head and spend time with other people. Maybe that would make me feel better?"

Dustin nodded. "Yeah, probably. You haven't really had a group of friends since we moved after Juniper was born."

"I wanted to, I just..."

"You've been preoccupied as a housewife and a stay-at-home mom. And honey, you have anxiety." Dustin said this last bit with a gentle sweetness. It was a gentle justification, not a ridicule. "You're not going to be the kind of person to make friends with strangers at the park. And that's okay. But maybe the witchcraft thing and the art contest will help push you out of your comfort zone and expose you to more people."

"Maybe," she thought, a little nervous at the thought of adding the pressure of "making friends" to the art contest. "I should see how Monday goes first, though."

She covered the page with a soft lilac color. The two options in watercolor technique are either background to foreground or lightest to darkest. This was a mix of both since the background was also a light color. As she let that dry, she started sketching on the back of junk mail some potential designs for the ten of pentacles card that was going to be the focus of the piece.

Sunday went by in a blur. They took the kids to the beach after breakfast for a few hours since it was only a 45-minute drive away. Selene had packed a picnic for lunch, after which they drove home. Juniper fell asleep in the car and continued napping when they got home. Sterling and Dustin played with Legos, and Selene painted. After Juniper woke from her nap, the family started prepping for the week. Dustin signed Sterling's permission slip to go to an apple orchard with his class, then he added some things he needed to the grocery list that Selene would get on Monday, and Selene prepped pancakes for the week and made the weekly meal plan.

Monday morning came quickly, too, and although she had a full day of chores to do, Selene was buzzing with anticipation for the full moon that night. She went to the grocery store and listened to a playlist someone had made that fit the vibes of this hunter's moon specifical-ly. She went home and lit her candle, the offering to the spirit of her home, and started prepping her vegetables. She knew that if she waited to chop onions or bell peppers, they would go bad before she got around to it. She chopped and diced and bagged the produce, storing them in the freezer except what she needed for tonight's dinner: chili and cornbread.

The meal was easy, but since she needed to be at the coven meeting for dinner, she wanted to make sure the family was taken care of before she left. The recipe was simple. It was mostly black, pinto, and kidney beans, some canned tomato, corn, diced onion and bell pepper, salsa, garlic, and broth. She poured it all into the slow cooker and set it to cook on low. She added some seasonings with magical intention. The cornbread muffins she would start later.

She took Conner out for a walk down to the creek and gathered some river water in a small jar. "River water is supposed to be good for letting things go," she told him, even though he was a dog. "I'm hoping it helps my creativity flow," she continued. "Get it... flow? Like a river?"

Conner wasn't paying her any attention, just panting happily and enjoying the breeze. On the walk back, she got a text from Jordan.

Jordan: Super excited to see you tonight! Bring your own container for moon water if you want to make some here.

Selene: Sounds good! I should have asked before, but is there like, a dress code?

Jordan: Not really. It's casual. Some people have ritual clothing they wear like robes and crowns, but if that's not part of your usual practice, then don't worry about it.

Selene wondered if she should have ritual clothes, and if she did, what would they look like as part of her regular practice? Since her practice was more focused on the home, maybe an apron? Her mind drifted. She had been wanting a nice, durable apron for a while. Should she learn how to make one? Could she thrift one? It would be nice to have, and she used to know how to cross-stitch, maybe she could embellish one with her kids' names?

Before she knew it, she was back home, and it was time to get the kids from school. Dustin was home, having grown bored scrolling through and applying for jobs. "I needed a break; a change of scenery. I applied to two more positions, but they aren't electrical jobs. We'll see."

"Do you mind picking up the kids today?" Selene asked. "I want to make the cornbread muffins and get some painting in before the ritual tonight."

"Sure thing, I'll leave in a minute."

Selene got the jar of river water and placed it on the kitchen table with her other painting supplies. She mixed the cornbread batter and popped it in the oven, then stirred the chili in the slow cooker. Then she sat down at her watercolors. She dipped her brush into the river water, "Please wash the stress away and just let me enjoy this," she asked the water. Conner scratched behind his ear. Dustin was in the bedroom, and Selene could hear him putting on his shoes.

She took a deep breath and then painted. She lost herself in it, pausing only to receive a kiss from Dustin as he left. She added pigment slowly, not wanting to make the color too harsh too quickly. When she needed to pause and let a section dry, she worked on the design for the tarot card.

It was difficult. She wanted it to hide ten literal pentacles in it, while also composing another image. Her first thought was stones on a path, but the pentacles ended up looking like the melting clocks painting. She felt stuck on the card's design but was making progress on the painting itself. It was probably the best work she had done to date.

She saw the car pull up from her kitchen window. She hurriedly put everything away and got out the cheese block to shred for dinner. "Mom!" Sterling shouted as he came inside. He and Juniper ran to her and hugged her.

"Hey, you guys," she smiled. She loved it when they got home.

"Daddy picked me up in the car," Sterling said. "No walk today."

"I see that," Selene said. Dustin shrugged. Juniper had a bandage on her forehead. "What happened here?"

"She fell into a chair outside, tripping on a rock," Dustin filled her in.

"I have owie," Juniper said, pointing at her forehead. "I fall down."

Selene gave her little girl a hug. "Can I kiss it?" Juniper nodded, and Selene gave her a kiss right on the bandage. "You're so strong."

"Big and strong like me," Sterling said. Then he played with Conner, and Juniper joined him.

"Everything is ready for dinner," she told Dustin. "Chili in the slow cooker, and these cornbread muffins are for tonight. Top the chili off with sour cream and cheese in the individual bowls."

Dustin nodded and ran a hand across her shoulders. "Go get ready, you need to leave soon," he told her.

She went to her room and grabbed her tarot cards, a jar for the moon water, and tucked a rose quartz in her bra. She also put her book of shadows in her bag. Back in the kitchen, she grabbed the grocery bag containing moon pies, store-bought and not homemade, which was not what she preferred, but it would have to do.

The drive was about 40 minutes, so she listened to the radio and felt her nerves climb as she got closer and closer to her destination.

Chapter Eight

Jordan lived in a small house in an older neighborhood, the kind where each house looked like it was an individual design. Selene liked the lack of uniformity. The house had a huge tree in the front behind a short chain link fence, and there were, from what Selene could tell, three chickens wandering the property. There was a huge peace sign woven out of branches that was attached above the garage door.

Selene: I'm here.

Jordan: Yay! I'll be right out.

By the time Selene got out of the car and grabbed her purse and the bag of moon pies, Jordan had materialized in her driveway. She greeted Selene with a hug and a hearty, "Come on back!"

They went through the side gate to the right of the house opposite the front door. This fence was wooden, and Jordan bolted it shut once they were inside the backyard.

"My sister-in-law is watching my kid inside," Jordan offered. "Which is great because now I can focus on the circle and the baby gets time with Auntie, which they both love."

"Your sister-in-law doesn't practice?"

Jordan laughed. "No. I think she's scared of it a little bit, but that's okay. She knows the invitation is always open."

In the backyard, there was a cast iron fire pit above a concrete pad with a few collapsible chairs around it and a table full of covered food.

There were two people. One Selene couldn't see except for their red cloak, who sat in a chair and was turned facing away from her and toward the other person. She was a woman in her thirties on a yoga mat in a deep lunge with her arms straight up above her head. They both turned towards Selene and Jordan when Jordan announced, "Ladies, this is Selene."

The one in the chair was a bigger woman; she looked like she could stop a car with just a look or with her strength. She had a buzz cut that was so short she could be considered bald, with a woven metal diadem on her head. The delicate wires were wrapped in such a way that they had the shape of three peaks.

Both women smiled and waved, saying hello. Awkwardly, Selene held up the shopping bag and said, "I brought moon pies!"

"Oh, that's great!" Yoga Mat said with the sound of a southern accent. "I like somethin' sweet after castin'."

She moved positions, bearing weight on her hands and feet, her head down and rump up like an upside-down V. "My name is Annette, pardon me for not greetin' you properly, I just need a good stretch in after work before I can be really present here with y'all."

"Oh, that's okay," Selene said. "What is it that you do?"

"I'm a private investigator. Most of my clients are actually family law attorneys, having me dig up dirty work for their clients."

"Don't get her started," the cloaked woman teased, "she's a bona fide workaholic."

"This is Liz," Jordan said.

Liz laughed, "Oh, yeah, that's me," then she looked at Jordan, "and Karina just got off work, she's on her way." Selene suddenly felt very self-conscious about her employment status.

"Great, she won't be too long then," Jordan smiled.

"Karina needs to quit that place before something bad happens," Annette said between stretches. "I swear, I don't even need to start diggin' to tell you that the owner is sketchy. You can just see it in her body language. The whole restaurant is probably a scam."

"Karina works as a server at Sushi Sun," Liz told Selene. "Come, sit down, I don't bite, at least not for free." Everyone except Selene laughed at some inside joke she hadn't learned.

Jordan touched her gently on the arm, "Go ahead and make yourself comfortable, Selene. I'll be right back." Then she turned and went inside.

"Well, I'll be interested to see how long they stay open after tax season. As a business, they just don't seem to be doing things right. Always messing up her paychecks?" Liz shook her head with a disapproving *humph*, "It's just fishy."

"And not just because it's sushi," Annette joked.

Selene laughed at the pun. "Do you have a lot of business experience?" she asked Liz. "I don't know anything about it, personally."

"Technically, I'm an independent contractor."

"For like, construction?" Selene could picture Liz building houses or doing maintenance. She looked strong, durable. Annette let out a hoot of laughter.

"No." Liz wore a small smile. "I work in the sex industry. I'm a dominatrix."

"Oh." Selene didn't know how to respond to that and hoped the blushing she felt wasn't visible in the light of the fire.

"Men pay me to bully them, and they like it. Some women, too. A lot of women pay me to be mean to their husbands, and they watch. It's all very empowering."

"For you," Annette said.

"Yes, for me." Liz sighed contentedly. "And the wives, too. Emasculating for the men, but they enjoy it."

Jordan came back out then, reading a text on her phone. "Dee and Paula won't be able to make it tonight," she said. "They're leaving early in the morning to visit Paula's parents, and they need to finish packing still."

"Aww that sucks," Annette said, "You came at the perfect night then, we would have been one person short if not for you."

Selene felt that too high an expectation needed to be met now. "I've never actually done a big formal casting ritual before," she confessed. Annette gave Jordan a curious look that subtly asked *did you clear this one?* "I'm a lot more casual with my practice," Selene continued.

"Selene is a hedge witch," Jordan offered, and then to make things even, shared, "Liz is a devotee of Lilith, Annette is a follower of Loki, and Freya from the Norse pantheon. If Dee and Paula were here, they're our two Wiccans, and Karina is... new."

"She's a baby witch," Annette said with glee as she put away her yoga mat. "She's still finding her way like a little bird that flew out of the nest."

"And she just pulled up," Liz said, reading a notification from her smart watch. Jordan went to open the gate to the backyard.

"Hey, sorry I'm late," said a young Hispanic woman. She had to be no more than 23 years old with straight, brown hair pulled back into a high, sleek ponytail. She wore all black pants, a V-neck top, and the telltale non-slip black shoes that were a staple of the food industry. In her hands were two large Styrofoam to-go boxes. "I brought egg rolls!"

"Yay, she made it!" Annette said.

"Let's get this party started," Jordan declared. "Alright Selene," Jordan started then stopped. "Oh, Karina, this is Selene. Selene, this is Karina." The two waved and smiled small smiles from such quick introductions. "Okay, so, Selene. You're new so you get to pick first."

Selene followed Jordan and everyone else to a picnic table in the grass. There were a few different colored candles and a caddy of herbs. It took a minute for her to realize everyone was waiting for her to do something. "I'm sorry, what?"

"Oh," Jordan smiled, "That's okay. We each hold a candle that corresponds to an element and invite them to join us when we cast the circle. You can pick whichever one appeals to you most: earth, air, fire, water. You can do spirit too if you'd like, but that one is usually the person who calls in all the others, so I don't know if you want to do all that."

Selene took a deep breath and looked past Jordan at the flames in the fire pit. The warmth and the colors were so comforting. She thought about her candlestick offerings back in her kitchen, and wondered at how the element of fire was such a comfort to her. Flickering candles, the warmth of freshly baked goods, the heat of summer. But water, especially watercolors and the creek she walked Conner to, and the pool of their apartment complex *also* brought a sense of cool peace.

"Fire, I think," she finally said.

Jordan handed her the red pillar candle and gestured to sit on one of the benches of the picnic table. "Everyone else, remember to grab a candle different from the one you did last time." Annette sat next to Selene and everyone else sat on the opposite bench. There remained a blue, green, yellow, and purple candle. "We are made up of all the elements, not just one. So, we need to honor them all equally."

Liz grabbed blue, Annette took yellow, and Karina looked between purple and green. "You can cast the circle tonight if you want to," Jordan encouraged her. Karina shook her head.

"Maybe next time," Karina said, selecting the green candle. Jordan took the remaining candle, purple, for spirit.

"Alright, I am going to talk us through the prep work. Group circle means group effort and group energy. I am not casting this circle on my own; we are all putting our magic into it." She reached into the caddy and pulled out a few sharpened sticks. They were almost like pencils, but twigs and small branches carved to have a point, no lead or graphite inside. "Everyone is going to dress their candles. You can carve into it any words, sigils, or symbols that correspond with the element."

Selene carved the word "FIRE" in big letters down one side and drew some flames. She added the symbols for Aries, Leo, and Sagittarius, the three fire signs in Astrology.

"I don't know what kind of words to put," Karina said.

"Well, water deals with emotion, fire with creativity, air with intellect, and earth with materialism," Jordan said, "That's not a bad thing, it could mean finances and security, comfort and possessions."

"You could also write things like roots and growth," Selene offered.

"After carving your candles, dress them with the anointing oil. Make sure you start at the wick and pull it down toward the base. This draws the energy in. If you want, you can then add some herbs. The bottles have little labels on them for popular correspondences, if that helps. I also have some glitter because I love it."

"What do you use as anointing oil?" Annette asked. "I usually buy some in a bottle at The Wayward Mart online, but I want to save money."

"I use olive oil," Liz said. "I just bless it first."

"That's what this is," Jordan said. "I figured, if it's good enough to eat, it's good enough for me."

Selene added some oil to her candle. It was smooth and rich; she stroked it down and thought it would be nice to occasionally dress up the candles in her home. Then she added calendula flower and golden glitter.

When everyone was done, Jordan told them each where to stand. There were four small tables surrounding the fire pit in a twenty-five-foot diameter. Each one was in one of the four cardinal directions, and Selene was in the South for fire. Jordan went around and cleansed everyone with a selenite wand.

"Selene-night!" Annette said, another pun. "Because it's Selene's first night."

Jordan waved the wand over each person's body, similar to that of a TSA agent with a handheld metal detector.

"Let us begin," Jordan decreed. She was in the middle of the circle and had put on a lilac cloak. She held a white taper candle, much taller and thinner than the pillar candles they each held for the elements. The purple candle was placed on a small table near the fire pit. Jordan lowered the white taper candle to the flames and lit the wick, then she walked over to Karina. Selene's entire body was thrumming with anticipation.

"Earth," Jordan's voice rang out clear and as smooth as olive oil, "we summon you from the east. We thank you for our home, our bodies themselves. Join us, and welcome."

"Join us and welcome," Karina said as Jordan lit the green pillar candle in her hands with the taper candle. Karina set the green candle on her small table, which was adorned with crystals. Selene thought of the rose quartz in her bra, touching her body. Earth to earth.

Jordan moved toward Annette. "Air, we summon you from the North. We thank you for the breath in our lungs. Join us and welcome."

"Join us and welcome," Annette repeated. When her yellow candle was lit, she placed it on a small table with burning incense.

Then, instead of moving around to Liz in the west, Jordan cut across to Selene. Her palms started sweating. *Please don't drop the candle,* she thought to herself. "Fire, we summon you from the south!" Jordan called out once she was right in front of Selene. "We thank you for the passion within us, the warmth of being alive. Join us and welcome."

"Join us, and welcome," Selene said as she had seen the others do. Jordan gave her a private smile as she lit the red pillar candle, and the flame danced above the red wax, burning down the wick. Selene turned south and placed it on the little table, which had three other tea light candles on it.

Jordan moved along to Liz with the blue candle. "Water, we summon you in the West. Thank you for sustaining us. Join us and welcome."

"Join us and welcome," Liz echoed. The blue candle was lit and placed on a pedestal within a bowl of water so the candle would not be submerged.

Jordan went to the center of the circle to the purple candle. "Spirit, we summon you! From within each and every one of us, thank you for the connection to each other and the universe within and beyond. Join us, bind us, and welcome!"

"Join us and welcome," everyone said, Selene a moment behind, picking up the cue.

"I call earth to bind the spell, air to speed its travel well, bright as fire shall it glow, deep as tide of ocean flow, and with the fifth, the circle shall hold," Jordan chanted. "The circle is now closed. Sentinels, you can rest from your posts and move freely."

Selene watched everyone relax and make their way to the chairs around the fire.

"As with every Full Moon, it's a great time for a forgiveness ritual. With the moon's face fully illuminated, we should also illuminate some of those dark, hidden spaces within us. Those spaces where we might be holding on too tightly to wrongdoings of ourselves or others, any grief, guilt, or shame. Tonight is the night to forgive and let those things, those frustrations, go." Jordan looked at each person sitting around the fire. "I'm not saying forgiveness means you need to rebuild burnt bridges. I'm not saying you need to form connections with someone who has hurt you, but I am saying that those past hurts can stop. You don't have to carry them anymore." Jordan produced some clipboards with blank computer paper on them and pens. "You cannot bring in new until you chuck out the old. You cannot manifest a good life for yourself if you refuse to relinquish the bad parts you want to get rid of. For your own peace, let's let that shit go."

Once everyone had a clipboard, she also handed out mason jars of ice water. "Here, drinks in case you get thirsty. Now, there's no right way to do this. Maybe you want to write out your forgiveness as a list. Maybe you want to start with a list of the things you need to let go of and then write down more about each one. Maybe it's a letter to a deity or ancestor, or a letter to a specific person who hurt you. Maybe it's a letter to yourself or a combination of all of it. Write it down and release it. No one will read it. When you are done, toss it in the fire and watch it burn away."

"From my hands to the fire," Liz said, slightly dazed, staring unblinkingly into the fire.

Everyone started writing. Jordan and Annette wrote at a moderate pace. Liz wrote slowly, often staring introspectively at the flames. Karina was scribbling with zealous abandon. Selene looked at her own paper. Forgiveness. What did she need to forgive? What did she need to let go of? She thought about it and after a few minutes, she began to write.

I love my life. I really do. But sometimes I miss who I was before I was a mom. There's a kind of grief to it. I would never want to go back to before. Never would I choose to, but sometimes I miss that version of me. She had friends, she had fun. I'm lonely a lot of the time. My husband is at work, not currently, but still, he's off job hunting. My kids are at school. I do chores around the apartment and take my dog for walks, and that's kind of it. That's my whole life sometimes. And I know that there's more to it. I have my practice, this coven is new for me, but I used to have girls I could call at any time. Then, when Sterling was born, most of them just stopped inviting me out. I would invite them over, and they would bail. That transition into motherhood was so reformative to who I am, I guess some friends just don't care to watch you grow.

So I forgive them. I forgive them for staying the same; it's not up to them to change just because I did. I forgive them for letting the gap between us expand beyond our reach. And I forgive myself. After Juniper was born and we moved, I didn't try as hard to find new friends. I hid within my anxiety, and I kept myself isolated. I want my family to be my all, but we are made for more human connections than that. I forgive myself for taking this long to take a leap into a group of people. I didn't know what to expect when I drove here tonight, but I already feel so connected to these women. I release the guilt and shame I have carried related to being lonely. And I want to release it from other aspects too. I feel embarrassed that I am a stay-at-home mom, that I don't make any money. Especially now that Dustin is out of work. I can't help but chastise myself that if I were working, we wouldn't be so scared. I wouldn't be so scared. I worried about our finances a lot, even before Dustin was let go. We were making it by, but we weren't as comfortable as we wanted. He tells me that I do so much for the family, that the work I do is too important... but what can I do to help? And even if I could, I feel tormented that I would be away from my kids when they need me. So, if I am unwilling to change the availability I have to my family, then I need to let go of the shame I have that propels me into possibly joining the workforce. I forgive myself for measuring my happiness and success against a life I don't even want for myself.

And Dustin, I love him. I know it's not his fault that we are in this predicament. I just wish he took my concern more seriously. I feel like he's too comfortable, too confident that we are going to be okay, that it makes me feel crazy for worrying. I know he doesn't mean to minimize my concern. I forgive him for that anyway, and I forgive myself for worrying. I release the worry and embrace the joy that he has, the confidence in my husband, and his job hunt.

Finally, the art contest. I don't want to become so blinded by winning that I lose my creative spirit. I release the pressure to win - but is it okay to still want to win? To still hope for it? Even if I can release the pressure of expectation, I still want to do my best and be proud of my work.

After about twenty minutes of writing, Jordan folded her paper once and tossed it into the fire. She mumbled something under her breath that Selene couldn't hear, but then in her normal voice said, "If you want to, you can invoke a spirit, deity, or whatever before surrendering your forgiveness to the fire to burn away the things weighing you down."

Liz followed suit, but instead of whispering, just said, "Lilith." She dropped in her paper and walked over to the blue candle.

Annette and Karina were still writing, so Selene stood up and put the clipboard on her chair. She folded the paper and held it to her heart for just a moment, feeling the rose quartz in her bra press against her sternum. "To myself, the magic in me, and the universe," she whispered. Then she let the paper go into the fire. She watched it for a moment as the fire caught, burning along the edges first, curling them inward as the flames crawled toward the center, the paper being reduced to white hot ash.

When everyone was done and returned to their positions, Jordan began releasing the elements in reverse order – spirit, water, fire, air, then earth. Jordan was letting them know that they were free to leave, but welcome to stay as the circle was opened.

"The circle is open but never broken," she declared. "Merry meet, merry part, and merry meet again!"

"Merry meet, merry part, and merry meet again!" they replied. The moment settled over them, and Selene savored it. It was therapeutic, the release under the Full Moon, and even though she had just met them, she knew there was something special forming in this group. A group that now included her.

"Let's eat," Annette said, breaking the silence. Liz and Jordan lifted the picnic table and moved it closer to the fire. The food table was covered in mismatched foods, but Selene was suddenly so hungry that it didn't even matter that none of it went together. Egg rolls, moon pies, Annette's casserole, Liz's fruit kabobs, and Jordan's butternut squash pasta. They served themselves buffet style on paper plates and sat at the picnic table.

"I feel better," Karina said. "I was carrying a lot of resentment toward my ex, and I don't really need to anymore. Also," she held up a moon pie. "These are so good. I can't believe I had never had one before."

"I thought it would be funny, because the moon..."

"Oh my god," Annette said. "That's punny, I'm keeping you."

Selene blushed. "I want to find a recipe to make my own for next time. I like homemade things, I just didn't think of moon pies until this afternoon."

"Next time, eh?" Jordan said, one eyebrow raised. "Would you want to come back?"

"You have to come back," Annette said.

"Liz didn't scare you off?" Karina said, surprised.

"I behaved," Liz said proudly.

"One of the things I wrote about related to how I need and want a community in my life outside of my family unit," Selene confided. "I really feel connected right now, and I haven't felt this way in a while."

"Well, you're one of us now," Liz said.

"Yeah, you can't get rid of us," Annette said, playfully bumping their shoulders together.

Selene could have floated from the love and support she felt. Acceptance.

"Well, when are we next meeting?" Karina asked, "Halloween is the day before the New Moon, and we can have two meetings in a row, but that feels excessive. And I would need to request the days off work."

"I'm taking my kid trick-or-treating at Fall Fest," Selene said. "Sterling really wants to be a dragon this year. I haven't even started working on finding a costume for him."

"We can meet once because the energy will carry over," Jordan said. "And I don't want to disrupt anyone's plans with family, and I know I want to take my kiddo out for trick-or-treating too. So let's meet the night after? On the New Moon."

"Sounds good to me," Liz said.

"Sure," Annette agreed. "I'm looking forward to Fall Fest, too. They've got the best pumpkin pies."

Everyone hummed in agreement. "I actually, uh," Selene hesitated without knowing what held her back, but she shook it off and pushed through, "I am thinking about maybe entering the art contest."

They all looked at her so much more excited than she thought they would be.

"Details!" Karina exclaimed.

"Yeah, spill," Jordan said with sarcastic annoyance that gave the impression that she knew that Selene had been holding back on them.

"I'm working on a watercolor piece," she said, then got more excited to share the secret of it. "It's also kind of a spell for financial security because I'm using river water to wash away concern and have money *flow* in." Annette nodded, and Liz looked impressed.

"I love that," Karina said.

Selene pushed through her hesitation to continue again; she wanted to be open with these women. They were welcoming her and accepting her, she could tell them the truth. "I'm a stay-at-home mom, so I don't have an income, and my husband carries the burden of providing for us. But he was recently let go from his last job due to downsizing, and he's looking for work." After a few tsks and sympathetic noises from the group, Selene kept going. "He has had a few interviews but no job offers just yet. He's an electrician, and he's really trying to find work in his field. I'm trying to be patient, but it's already been two weeks, which was the pay covered by the severance package. He's, well, we, are hopeful. Nervous, but hopeful."

"I think it's cool you found a way to combine art with your craft," Liz said.

"Oh my god," Annette said, "Arts and Crafts!" Everyone started giggling.

"I'm putting that on friendship bracelets for us now," Karina said.

"What's your painting of?" Jordan asked.

Selene pursed her lips. "It's a surprise."

"Come on now, Jordan," Liz chastised, "you can't spoil it! We're all going to see it and be super proud of our Selene."

"Well, I haven't actually signed up yet," Selene confessed.

"When is the deadline?" Annette asked.

"Tomorrow."

"Witch," Jordan scolded. "If you don't sign up right now," she stood up and walked toward her back door. "I'm getting my laptop and you," she pointed at Selene, "are committing to this thing."

A few moments later, the coven was gathered around Selene as she filled out the art contest registration form on Jordan's laptop.

"And, submit," she said as she clicked the cursor over the final button. The women cheered.

"Time for a toast!" Jordan decreed, and she opened a bottle of sweet red wine and poured everyone a glass. It was bubbly and light, which was exactly how Selene was feeling. They chatted more and snacked.

"New moon rituals are so fun," Liz told Selene. "We make vision boards and it's all about manifesting."

"But Jordan and Annette don't call them vision boards," Karina interjected, "they call them 'moon boards'. Cringe."

"Because it's the moon!" Annette protested.

"And it's for the one lunar cycle!" Jordan agreed, equally defensive.

"You guys are nerds," Liz said.

"And you love us for it," Jordan cooed. Liz just shrugged and sighed as if to say *what can you do*.

"Well, I need to get goin'. It's a work night," Annette said, finishing her mason jar of water. "Tomorrow, I need to be at this guy's house at the butt crack of dawn to see if his mistress is there when he heads out to work."

"Oo, do you think he will be?" Selene asked.

"Oh, probably, men tend to be idiots and his soon-to-be ex-wife's attorney asked me to get the scoop on the guy. Apparently, his legal team is stating that there is no mistress in some elaborate scheme so that he doesn't need to pay child support."

"Wow," Jordan said.

"Yeah, divorce court can get real messy. It's like trying to run a high school rumor mill. But these attorneys keep hiring me and they pay well."

"I should get going too," Selene said. "I want to get up before the kids do in the morning and try and give them extra time."

Jordan walked Selene out to her car. "I'm really glad you came," she said. "I think you're a great fit for the group."

"Thanks, I'm glad I did too. I," Selene paused, truly taking in how free she felt compared to when she arrived. Her anxieties and the weight of them were absent now. "I needed this."

Jordan opened her arms for a hug, and without hesitation, Selene stepped in and hugged her new friend back. It felt light and warm, the way a friend glues you together, the way only platonic connections feel – just good and right.

Chapter Nine

When she got home, Selene slid into bed next to her sleeping husband. Dustin wrapped an arm around her, half-awake. "I love you," he mumbled.

Selene spent every free moment on her watercolor painting, and Dustin prepared for his interview with the high school district.

One day, Selene's mom called to talk to Sterling and Juniper.

"I'm going to be a dragon for Halloween," Sterling told her. "Momma's helping me make my costume."

"Oh really?"

Sterling nodded seriously over the video call. "It has red wings and a crown with horns."

"Let Grandma talk to your mom."

Selene sighed and took the phone. "Hi, Mom."

"That sounds like a Devil costume," she snapped. No preamble, no *how are you doing*. Just instant criticism.

"It's not a devil costume, it's a homemade dragon costume. We made the wings out of cardboard, and he painted them himself. The horns are attached to an old crown from last year's king costume, but you can't see the crown."

Her mother looked annoyed, narrowing her eyes. "It's still satanic."

"It's a dragon, Mom."

"Are you at least taking them to a church event? It's important to protect the youth from the evil trappings out there on Halloween. That's when all the weirdos are out."

"Mom, we don't do church. You know that."

"It's never too late to start," she said. Despite the words themselves seeming like an invitation, the tone was hard, like a teacher who wouldn't accept excuses.

"We are going to the local Fall Festival. It's at the farm down the highway that has the big pumpkin patch. There's going to be a costume contest, a kids' party area, and trunk-or-treating."

"I don't like the idea of trunk-or-treating," her mother continued. "When you were little, we taught you not to accept candy from strangers in their cars."

"Is there anything else, Mom? I need to get dinner started."

"No, I was just calling to talk to the babies. Alright, I'll let you go. Dad and I want you to come up for Thanksgiving."

"Yeah, probably. Love you."

"Mmhmm, I love you too."

Selene hung up the phone and took a long slow breath.

Chapter Ten

O n the morning of his interview, Dustin turned to Selene and said, "You know, I've been thinking."

"Oh, that's dangerous," Selene joked.

"I have my interview today and I think we need something to look forward to." He raised his eyebrows and his hands. "What if we went down to the lake tonight?"

Well, the kids were within earshot, putting on their shoes for school, and Sterling was quick and assertive in his support of this plan. Seeing her brother's excitement, Juniper also got excited. Soon, all three of them were chanting "Lake night! Lake night! Lake night!" at Selene. Even Conner was trotting around in circles.

"Alright, alright," Selene laughed. "We will go to the lake tonight."

"Yay!" Their cheers filled the living room. Conner let out a single bark.

She spent the day continuing to work on her watercolor and some of the final touches. All that remained was the tarot card, which was continuing to prove more and more difficult to design in a way she liked.

When Dustin came home from his interview, he had brought the kids home with him. "I already packed us a picnic for dinner," Selene told them. "It's ready to go, I just need to get my shoes on."

"I want to change, too," Dustin said, taking off his tie on his way to their bedroom. "Sterling, put your backpack away, don't leave it on the floor."

"What's this, Mama?" Juniper asked, climbing up onto the kitchen chair to look at the watercolor supplies that were still out, the latest layer still drying.

"It's Mommy's art project," Selene said. "It's almost done. Is it pretty?"

Juniper nodded. "I can help!" She reached across for a paintbrush.

Selene bolted. "Oh, no!" She grabbed the paintbrush and placed it back in the cup, bristles up. "We don't touch, okay?" She gestured to the watercolor painting, the supplies, and everything on the table. "Thank you so much for wanting to help, but you can just let mommy do this by herself, okay?"

"Okay," Juniper said, dejected.

Selene tried to find something to redirect her two-year-old's focus. "You know what would be helpful? Can you grab Conner's leash?"

"Okay!" Juniper said, rushing to find it. She loved to help; she loved having tasks to complete.

"Alright, family!" Dustin called out as he came around the corner. "Let's go to the lake!"

Sterling came out of the kid's room wearing his dragon wings. "Mom, can I take these?"

"Not tonight, buddy."

They went down to the lake, which was connected to the creek Selene and Conner frequented on their walks. When they got there, they found a picnic table, and Selene set out the food and everyone ate. After, Sterling played fetch with Conner, Dustin and Juniper threw rocks into the water, and Selene took it all in. They stayed until well past sunset, with the moon high and waning and a chill settling into the air.

"Let's get them home," Dustin said. "We'll put them to bed and then have one-on-one husband and wife time?" Selene nodded and smiled.

Juniper was half asleep by the time they pulled up to their apartment. "I'll give her a quick bath in our shower; that way, Sterling can shower at the same time," Dustin said.

He got Juniper's bath started and Selene grabbed pajamas for both kids. She also turned on the white noise machine in their room. "Hey buddy, it's time to take a shower," Selene said, walking back out to the living room when she stopped dead in her tracks.

"I'm sorry," Sterling said. The table was covered in water. It was dripping down the side of the table into a puddle on a chair and on the floor. He had an entire roll of paper towels that he was trying to clean it up with. "I'm sorry," he repeated, a tremor in his voice, a quiver in his bottom lip. He started to cry. "It was an accident. I'm sorry, I'm sorry. I'm sorry."

Selene was speechless. She lifted the paper towels on top of her painting and saw the carnage left behind. The water seeped into the paper, causing all the pigment to blend into a weird amorphous bunch of blobs.

"Don't cry, Sterling," Selene said. "Just... go take a shower."

Sterling stood there and cried harder. Selene wanted to cry too; she wanted to scream. She wanted to comfort him.

Dustin came around. "What happened?" he asked, Juniper wrapped up in a towel in his arms. He saw the mess and looked at Sterling with the glare of a father. "What. Happened."

Sterling babbled for a minute. "I, it, I was trying to, trying to help, because mama made my costume, and she had paint out, and I wanted to add paint to my dragon wings." He continued to cry. Selene wanted to throw the wings away with all her hard work, but that's not how an adult was supposed to handle things.

"Were you supposed to touch that stuff?" Dustin asked.

"No."

"What were you supposed to be doing?"

Sterling continued crying, "Taking a shower."

"Go. Shower." Dustin commanded. Sterling took off. "I'm gonna put Junie's pajamas on and then put her down. Are you okay?"

Selene took a deep breath. "It's just water and paint."

But when he had gone into the kids' room, she let herself cry over the hard work she had wasted.

"I don't know what I'm going to submit for the art contest now," Selene told Dustin once they were lying in bed together, both kids asleep, Sterling being reassured that he wasn't a bad kid and yes, she still loved him.

"You have time," Dustin comforted her. "Like, a week and a half."

"I don't know."

"Make the same painting? You already did it once." It was a logical solution, but Selene didn't think she could do it. She had spent so long on it, and it would be impossible to make it look exactly the same. And she still didn't know what the tarot card would look like.

"I don't know," she said again. "Maybe. I need to go for a walk tomorrow and get more river water. I'll make something."

Dustin kissed her. "It'll be great."

"At the very least, it will be. It will exist."

So, the next day, when Selene went down to the river to collect water for her painting, she looked around. She had thought about painting something like a riverscape with Conner in it, but that would be a lot of detail. Maybe, with the new time restriction, she would need to make something more interpretive instead of a rendering of a still life moment.

She texted Jordan:

Selene: Want to get together?

Jordan: Sure! Want to meet at the park?
I need to get out of the house.

Selene: Okay.

Selene took Conner with her to the park, and on the way there, she grabbed a green tea lemonade. She sat on the bench, Conner next to her ankle, laid down in the soft grass. She missed the days of bringing Sterling and Juniper here. Now they were both in school and daycare.

"Hey, Selene!" Jordan called out from the other side of the park.

She had her kid in a baby swing, so Selene walked over.

"Hey girl," Jordan said, giving her a hug. "How are you doing?"

Selene took a deep breath. "Well, Sterling spilled water on my painting so it's ruined. Dustin still hasn't gotten a job offer. And I don't know if it matters that I try hard on things because it's all frivolous and doesn't really make a difference."

"If it matters to *you*, then it matters," Jordan said. Selene gave a half-hearted shrug. It was not so different from what she would tell someone in her situation. "The painting can't be saved?"

"Nope, I have to start over. And I don't even know if I want to or if I should."

"Why not?"

Selene took a sip of her drink and contemplated how to respond. Jordan gave her the time. "Because," Selene said after a minute. "I can't go back and repaint the same thing. I mean, I could, but there's no joy in it now. It would just be me trying to replicate what I had already done."

Jordan gave her a look. "So paint something else."

"It's not that easy," Selene protested, feeling a bit petulant.

"Why not?"

"I don't know what to paint! It has to be good enough to enter into the contest."

Jordan rolled her eyes. "Forget about the competition, just paint something for you. Something that you like. If you decide to enter it when it's done, and hear me when I say you shouldn't make that decision until after it's done, then you can follow that path when it appears. There's no sense in navigating a road you aren't on yet."

"Yeah, I'll figure it out," Selene said. She patted her thigh, and Conner jumped up onto his hind legs, resting his front paws just above her knee so she could pet him.

"He's such a good dog," Jordan said. "And thanks for meeting me here. I know you were the one who asked to meet up, but I was feeling stir-crazy. I needed to get outside and talk to another adult."

Selene laughed, "I know how that goes! I do miss when my kids were home, though. I used to take them on all these adventures during the week, and it was never crowded or busy. Now, Sterling is in school and Juniper is in daycare. And it's good for her, she gets to play all day and learn, and she has friends. She loves daycare, and it has helped so much with her speech delay. I can't pull her out of it now." She sighed. "It was paid for in my grandmother's will, too, so I don't even have to pay for it, thankfully. And I love having the time to myself. It's just... I feel like I don't do enough."

Jordan nodded, "I know what you mean, but also, you do a lot. You cook practically everything, you're always mending and creating things for your family, and you manage their schedules. I know you feel bad about it, but if it works for your family, then it works." Jordan left a pause to let her words sink in. "So Dustin is still looking for work?"

"Yep. He was cut from the running for the job at the prison, which was one of the ones he had put a lot of effort into. There is one more potential job with the high school district, and then a few jobs he applied to that he's overqualified for. So he's worried about those denying him."

"I'll light a candle for him, try and ask the universe to help out a bit."

"Thank you," Selene said. Then she saw it, the idea for a painting. Five sets of hands, a collection of food that didn't seem to go together, and candles for each element. "I have an idea," she announced. Jordan smiled wide.

Chapter Eleven

Time blurred by, leaves fell to the ground, and the moon waned until it was but barely a sliver in the sky. Sterling's Halloween costume had its final touches of defined scales painted on, and Juniper's fairy wings were a great find at a thrift store. Before they knew it, it was the day of Fall Fest.

They loaded up for the festival and Juniper practiced how to say "Trick-or-Treat" and "Happy Halloween" in the back of the car. Selene and Dustin were dressed up as medieval townsfolk. "Hey there, Tavern Wench," Dustin said. "Come here often?"

"You want to help with that dragon, Sir Knight?" Selene countered with a smile. Sterling was overwhelmed with excitement and Juniper was looking around, taking in everything with her eyes wide. "I need to go take my painting to the art contest area, I think it's over by the stage for the costume contest."

"Okay," Dustin nodded, "Do you want to go alone or stick together?"

Sterling was pulling Juniper towards the little kids' center where there were bouncy balls that looked like jack-o-lanterns and bubble machines. "Dad, can we get candy?" he asked. Just beyond the play area was the entrance to the trunk-or-treat lot, where volunteers were passing out empty bags for the kids.

"One minute, kids. You go," Dustin told Selene, "Then let me know what the plan is. We can meet you in the trunk-or-treat lot."

Selene walked over to the stage, her painting framed but turned toward her in an attempt at secrecy. She didn't want to seem flashy, so she hid it as best she could as she approached the art contest table.

"Hi, I'm Selene Morret. I need to check in."

The gentleman at the table had long silver hair tied in a low ponytail. He checked her in and showed her where to hang her painting on the temporary walls erected by the Fall Fest for the contest.

"The adjudicators will make their rounds starting at 6 PM during the costume contest. They'll announce the winners at 8 PM on the main stage," the ponytail man informed her. "You don't need to be present to win; we send out emails to the winners anyway."

"Alright, sounds good," Selene said as she hung her painting on the wall.

"That's a really nice piece," he said, appraising the rendering. "I never could quite grasp watercolor, but I dig the way it looks."

"Thank you." She blushed, but she let herself feel the pride in her work.

Selene caught back up with her family by the trunk-or-treat lot. They walked through, and Sterling and Juniper loaded up their bags with candy. "We should save some for a Yule advent calendar," Selene said. "Plus the Mom and Dad Tax," Dustin said.

They ran into Jordan toward the end of the lot. She was Cruella De Vil, and her toddler was a Dalmatian. "I love your costumes!" Jordan exclaimed.

"I'm a dragon!" Sterling told her.

"I see that. What a powerful dragon you are." Then she looked at Selene. "Let's find the girls; they were getting pumpkin pie. We all want to see your painting!"

Selene's heart sped up just a bit, and her palms were sweaty as they walked over to the art display. Jordan was on the phone with Annette, telling her to get the coven over for the awards ceremony.

They were gathered in the back of the seating area.

"We saw your painting!" Karina said. "I want a print of it to hang up in my room."

"Me too," Liz said.

"Oh, I can put one in my office!" Annette chimed in.

There were two older ladies present as well. "This is Dee and Paula," Jordan introduced them.

"Nice to meet you," Selene said.

An announcer grabbed the microphone on the stage, "I hope everyone is having a good time." Selene turned and saw the ponytail man on stage with a clipboard in hand. "We are going to announce the winners of the art contest. There were a record-breaking 89 entries.

We have prizes for first, second, and third place, but before we announce that, let's get a round of applause for all our entries and our judges!" Applause sounded throughout the seating area. "In third place, Kris Grains!" Applause as a young man climbed the stage with a projection behind him of his painting: a field with a scarecrow. "In second place, Selene Morret!" Her support group erupted. Selene was shocked as she walked up the steps. Her blood was pumping in her ears as she received an envelope and a handshake. She had won. She had *won*. Maybe not first place, but she had placed in her first contest ever, and she had an amazing group of people cheering for her. Her family and her coven. It didn't solve everything, but she knew that everything was going to be okay.

Chapter Twelve

A few days later...

Selene was wiping down the counters after re-setting the kitchen. The dishwasher running, the candle glowing steady on the counter, her watercolor painting of the coven table dressing candles on the wall beside the dining table. She got a call from Dustin. "Hello?" she answered.

"Hey, babe, I'm off early today, so I'll pick up the kids on the way home."

"How was your first day?" she asked.

"It was great." She could hear his smile. "I think it's going to be a really great job. And the high school is just across the street from Juniper's daycare, so it's really convenient. Oh, and there's going to be an office Friendsgiving party next week. What do you want to make for that?"

Selene looked around her kitchen. "Pumpkin pie," she said.

There are some things that every witch worth her salt knows. One of these is the benefits of cinnamon. Prosperity, luck, abundance, you name it.

Burn Me Down

A Powerful Woman Collection

What happens when time doesn't heal all wounds?

Everything between Corinne and Veronica went up in smoke. Their romance, their friendship, and even neutrality have turned to ash. These assassin witches take down their marks easily. Old feelings, however, are as hard to kill as each other.

As long as you want forever, you'll always taste nothing but me, Veronica Afilado.

Five years after their explosive end, Veronica and Corinne cross paths once again. They've shared more than a professional and personal history. Now that Veronica is running her mouth, Corinne curses her. Veronica retaliates. Thus begins a violent back-and-forth.

When the line between hate and desire is so blurred, how far is too far?

Inspired by Sabrina Carpenter's "Taste" lyrics and music video, Taste the Burn blazes with the heat of simmering rage and boiling passion.

Burn Me Down

A Powerful Woman Collection

A witch in hiding. A man seeking answers.
A love forged in fire.

Witch hunting never stopped, it just evolved. An evolution Morgan Winter experienced when her life was destroyed. Engulfed in grief, it is only with the help of her cat familiar, her sister-in-law, and her late husband himself that she starts to move on and love her life again.

When Killian Henderson arrives in her secluded town, she's drawn to him despite the hauntingly familiar danger in his scent. Partnered with his sister, he's searching for the truth about his family's past, but the truth is a nightmare.

As a forbidden attraction ignites, the past erupts into the present. To be together, they must choose between the legacy they inherited and the future they desire—before the flames of a generations-old feud consume them both.

Burn Me Down
A Powerful Woman Collection

At the Hearth is a cozy slice of life novella, focused on self-love, familial love, and the importance of community.

Selene loves her family and loves her home. A hedge witch and stay-at-home mom of two kids, she spends her days casting spells of protection, planning little adventures for the family, and picking up toys. As she tries to take care of her family amidst financial insecurity, her husband encourages her to explore herself and her craft outside her roles at home.

Her anxieties rage against her, but in a journey to find herself and a coven, the hedge witch paints a new path.

Burn Me Down

A Powerful Woman Collection

Amongst the oceans and trees of the Pacific coastline, Amelia is the last of her fading coven and their only hope. If she doesn't find a way to infuse more magic into the coven, the magic won't survive another generation. When her Grams comes to find her on the beach, she makes a request that changes everything for Amelia. If she can do what is being asked, her coven can see future generations of magic, but if she fails, they will have to disband and leave their magic behind.

Without hesitation, she agrees to try to save her people by uprooting her life. A new place, filled with new people, and her only comforts are the ocean and the library, but with knowledge comes power. Making friends or finding enemies, either way, she needs to uncover the truth before her wedding, or else she is bound to this man for the rest of their lives.

Acknowledgements

Thank you, Jacob. My partner in life, in parenting, in love, and in chaos. Thank you for never dropping my hand. Thank you, Hazel, for cuddles while I typed, for all the light you bring to my life. And thank you to Violet. I drafted this little cozy slice of life while 8 and 9 months pregnant with you, and I wrote "the end" just a few days before you were born. My little family, thank you for being my world.

Thank you to my friends at Mythic Royals! This collection is the first of its kind for me and I'm thrilled at the idea of more collaborations in the future. Thank you C. J. Willis and Chelsey J. León for being unhinged, to Lyss for editing, to Elisabeth Garner for formatting, cover art, and promo materials.

Shout out to my Street Team and my readers for hanging out in my corner.

About the Author

Stephanie Jean is a California author, veteran wife, and mother of two goblins. She has an Associate Degree in Paralegal Studies, a Bachelor's Degree in Theatre. Along with reading, her hobbies include community theatre, cross stitch, camping, video games, and going to museums, libraries, and parks. You'll probably find her streaming Monterey Bay Aquarium live streams or rewatching comfort shows.

Please take some time this week to go to your local library!

Join Stephanie Jean's newsletter mailing list for all the updates and insider knowledge on upcoming projects, events, and sales!

OTHER WORKS BY STEPHANIE JEAN

<u>Novels:</u>

Not a Showmance
Face the Music

✦ ✦ ✦ ✦ ✦ ✦ ✦

<u>Poetry:</u>

The Spell Jar: Book of Shadows
*one of many poets in the collection

9 798990 208346